Possessing Liberty

A Curvy Girl Military Romance

Nichole Rose

Nichole Rose

Copyright

Contents

Dedication

This one is for our service members. Thank you for all you do for those you've never met.

About the Book

FALLING IN LOVE NEVER *hurt so good.*

Killian

I'm a military man...rough, demanding, and used to being obeyed.

I don't do love. I don't date. I don't have time for either.

But Liberty Connor has me rethinking everything.

One kiss from those sweet lips, and I'm hers.

How do you convince an angel to fall for the devil?

You possess her.

Liberty

Killian Thorne is my worst nightmare.

Bossy, scarred...and hot as Hades.

He offered me a fortune to help him save vulnerable soldiers.

There's just one problem.

Who's going to save me from him when I fall hard for him and his rough ways?

Warning

This gruff former Marine isn't afraid to play dirty when it comes to his curvy younger woman. To convince her to fall, he'll teach her every wicked trick in the book. If instalove, heat, and over-the-top men make you sweat, get ready to fall for Killian and Liberty in this sweet, steamy romance from Nichole Rose. As always, a sticky sweet and guaranteed HEA are coming your way.

Chapter One

LIBERTY

"WHAT ARE YOU WORKING on?" Summer Alessi asks, plopping down in a chair across from my desk. She kicks her shoes off and curls her legs up underneath her, tugging on the hem of her floral Midi-dress to keep it from riding too far up her thighs. As usual, she looks gorgeous with minimal makeup and her red hair hanging in loose waves.

"The networking app," I mutter, blowing my hair out of my face and sitting back to peer at her through bleary eyes. I've been looking at my computer screen for so long I feel like my eyes are starting to cross. "It's driving me crazy. The algorithm is all wrong."

The stupid thing is supposed to match potential donors and volunteers with like-minded charities in their immediate area, but there's a glitch that keeps matching people with charities that don't align with their interests. We can't put it through a hard beta test until we get the algorithm issue fixed.

"Maybe Dominic can take a look at it for you," Summer suggests, referring to her new husband and my boss, Dominic Alessi. "He needs something productive to do. He's driving me crazy."

"Whatever," I say with a smile, not missing the sparkle in her eyes or the way she glows. Ever since Dom finally married her three months ago, she's been walking on cloud nine. "You love it when he's following you around."

Which he does all the time since they found out two weeks ago that she's pregnant. Watching our giant boss chasing her all around the building is hilarious. He's so adorably in love with her and their baby. Seeing them so blissed out makes me so happy for them.

Summer is a sweetheart, and Dom is an incredible boss. I've never had anyone look at me the way Dom looks at her and vice versa. I grew up in foster care and then spent my high school years in an all-girl's boarding school. At twenty-two, I know next to nothing about men or dating. But I know enough to know that Dom is head-over-heels for my best friend. He's been in love with her since the day she started working here. The only one who didn't know it was her, but they're past all that and gloriously happy now. They deserve it.

Summer grins at me, her entire expression lighting up. "I do love it," she admits with a little laugh. "I love everything about him."

"He feels the same about you. Where is he anyway?" I ask, rubbing my temples like that's going to stop the dull ache already prodding at me. I probably need to get my eyes checked but haven't had time to do it.

"In his office. He's meeting with a potential client."

"A nonprofit?"

"I don't think so," Summer says, her brows furrowed. "The client was kind of short on the phone and didn't say much. Just that he needs an app developed and someone recommended us. I tried to explain that we don't really do development for individuals, but he was insistent."

"Weird."

Summer shrugs. "Dominic agreed to see him. I guess he knows him or his brother or something. I don't know. He'll fill me in later. Do you want to get lunch while he's busy? I'm hungry."

"Is it already lunch time?" I glance at the clock on my computer and then curse beneath my breath. It's almost one. I've been at my desk for the last four hours straight. No wonder my head hurts and my eyes are tired.

"If I could hyper-focus like you do, I'd get so much done," Summer says, laughing at me. "You get busy and tune out the entire world."

"It's easy when you've done it as long as I have." I save my work on the program and then grab my wallet and keys out of my desk drawer. Growing up the way I did, I had to learn to tune out the world. It was the only way I ever got anything done over the sounds of the television blaring, the other kids playing, and the foster parents yelling. Once I was accepted into the boarding school, I worked hard to keep my scholarship so I didn't end up bouncing from home to home and school to school through high school. But I don't tell Summer that. I don't want her feeling sorry for me.

She reaches across the desk and squeezes my hand, sympathy welling in her baby blue eyes. She sees through me so easily. Most people don't. To them, I'm the smart, overweight girl who doesn't say much. I prefer it that way. But Summer had me pegged about three minutes after she walked in the door for the first time.

She's my best friend...my only friend, really. I don't get close to many people. But trying not to love Summer is impossible. She's genuine and has a heart the size of Texas.

"You have family now," she says, her voice soft. And then she squeezes my hand and drops the subject. "Can we have burgers? I'm craving fries soaked in ketchup."

"Sounds good to... Maybe not," I mutter when my desk phone lights up. I shoot Summer an apologetic grimace and then grab it. "Liberty Connor."

"Hey, it's Dom. Can you come to my office, please?"

"Now?"

"Yeah. I've got a project for you."

"Um, yeah, sure."

"Thanks."

He hangs up on me.

I frown, replacing the receiver. "Your man needs me in his office," I tell Summer. "Rain check on lunch?"

"Fine, but tell him he owes me French fries," she says, pouting. We both know he'll get them for her. He'd do anything to make her happy. She hops up from her seat, slipping her feet back into her ballet flats. "I'll order us takeout. You want your usual from *Andy's*?"

"Yeah." I slide my chair back and stand up, adjusting my black Peplum top. It's creased where I've been sitting so long, but there's nothing I can do about that now. There's nothing I can do about the fact that I'm wearing minimal makeup and faded jeans with strategically placed holes either. I wasn't expecting to meet with anyone today, so I dressed down. Hopefully, the potential client won't hold it against us.

Summer ducks out of my office and goes right. I take a left, headed toward Dom's office in the back corner. Most of the developers and engineers are on the second floor, but he moved me down to the first floor when Summer started. At first, I thought it was because I'm the youngest developer here and the only female of the bunch, but now I think he did it so she'd have a friend close. I think it's cute how he's always looked for little ways to make her happy, even before he found out that she loved him too.

He's so good to her.

"You needed to see me?" I say, poking my head inside Dom's office to find him ensconced behind his antique desk, his sleeves rolled up his forearms and his dark head bent while he jots notes on his tablet.

Whoa. I blink when I catch sight of the man sitting across the desk from him. The sun shining in through the windows hits him like a halo, making him look like an avenging angel come down to earth to mete out justice in the name of God. He's...massive. And entirely too handsome. His dark hair is crewcut, his eyes crystalline blue. His features are sharp, masculine. Not even the little lines around his eyes and mouth, the scruff on his jaw, or the wicked scar that bisects his right cheek detract from how gorgeous he is. If anything, they add to the appeal, giving him a dangerous, warrior vibe.

He flicks his gaze in my direction almost dismissively, and then he freezes. His brows climb, something dark flaring in those crystalline depths. I feel his gaze like a touch as it climbs up my body. I grip onto the doorjamb like that's going to keep me from fidgeting as desire shoots through me.

His gaze comes to rest on my breasts, his expression turning almost ravenous. Part of me wants to cross my arms and hide them like I have so many times in the past.

He's not the first man to stare blatantly at my boobs. I wear an H cup, making them impossible to miss. But he is the first man to make me wonder what it would feel like for him to play with them or sink his teeth into them.

I've been a big girl my entire life. There aren't a lot of men out there who have shown an interest in me, and none of them ever caught my eye. I've been on two dates in my life, and neither was great. This man seems interested though.

He slowly lifts his gaze to mine, command crackling in his expression. There's something hard in his eyes, some small glint that tells me he's hiding entire volumes behind them. Even from across the room, I can tell he's used to being in charge, to being obeyed. He's king alpha and he knows it.

He practically commands me to look away first, to lower my gaze and accept his rule...but I don't. Seeing that look on his face sends some undiscovered urge soaring through me hot and fast. *Challenge.* I want to rattle that authority, rattle *him*. I don't even know why, but something in me demands it.

So I hold his gaze, not backing down.

The man's upper lip twitches into the tiniest of smiles, pulling the scar on his cheek taut. He lifts his chin the slightest bit, silently telling me he knows what I'm doing and why. That he likes it. That little hint of a smile completely changes his carved-from-granite features, eradicating what composure I have. He's gorgeous in the same way a wolf is, fearsome and powerful.

Dom clears his throat and I jump, losing eye contact. *Dammit.*

My gaze flies back to the mystery man, but it's too late. He's already won. The dark glint in his eyes tells me that he knows it too.

"Liberty, this is Killian Thorne," Dom says, motioning for me to come in. "Killian, this is Liberty Connor, the software engineer I was telling you about."

"She's hired," Killian says, his gravelly voice a sharp crack of sound. "But she'll be working out of my office for the duration of the project."

Hired? Working out of his office?

Yeah, no.

I don't care how hot he is, no one but me decides where I work.

"*She* is standing right here," I tell him, standing up straight and squaring my shoulders. "And *she* will decide whether or not she wants to work with you and where she'll do that work."

A flash of...something crosses Killian's face, there and gone so quickly I almost miss it. It's dark and wicked, making him look more like a predator staring at his prey than a man offering me a job. Before I can even process that or what it means, the moment is gone.

"My apologies, Ms. Connor," he grits out. "Of course the choice is yours."

"Now that we're all on the same page," Dom says, his tone wry and slightly amused, "why don't you have a seat, Liberty? I think you'll be interested in the project Killian has for you."

I hesitate a split second before curiosity wins out. Dom knows me almost as well as Summer does. He knows the kind of projects I jump at and why. If he thinks hearing Killian out is worth my time, I should probably listen.

Killian watches me like a hawk as I cross Dom's office and take the only remaining seat, which is right beside Dom's desk. Killian grunts, a hint of irritation flitting through his expression before he schools it. That little flicker confuses me. Is he annoyed that I'm sitting beside Dom?

He keeps his eyes glued to me, assessing and considering, the entire time I get comfortable. Jeez, he's intense. And even hotter up close. There are flecks of gray in his eyes and the lines around his eyes are deeper than I first thought. He's maybe thirty-five or forty. The scar on his cheek looks old, but I can't help but wonder what happened to him.

I'm guessing he's military or law enforcement, someone used to barking orders and being obeyed without question. It would explain his curt demeanor, that scar, and the way he watches me like he sees more than everyone else.

I've never been a rule breaker, but a little part of me thrills at the thought of breaking his rules just to see how he reacts. Just to see him discomposed, that iron will of his eradicated. I can almost imagine those big hands clamped around my hips while he drives into me...almost feel the weight of them coming down across my ass as he punishes me with pleasure for some misdeed.

I clear my throat, trying to dislodge that image and the breathlessness it leaves behind. What am I even thinking? I'm a virgin. I wouldn't even know what to do with a man like him. He's gruff, rude...way too hot. I don't know what to do with any of that.

Part of me wishes I did.

"Um, tell me about this project," I murmur, my cheeks heating when I see the little hint of humor in his eyes like he knows exactly what I was thinking about, what I was imagining. It takes every ounce of willpower I have to keep from fidgeting beneath the weight of his stare.

He watches me for another moment, not speaking. "Need your help coding an application that'll match vets with services," he says then. The gravel-like quality of his voice should be a turn-off, but something about that deep, dark timbre sends a ripple of desire through me. "Lots of good men out there need help transitioning back to being a civilian."

He's not wrong about that. Men and women returning from overseas often find it hard to reacclimate to life as a civilian. My father was one of them. Eventually, he turned to alcohol and then to drugs. He lost custody of me, and then died not long later. I was seven when he passed away. I can't quite remember what it was like to have a parent, but I miss him in the way you miss an arm or a leg. It's a phantom pain, one that never really heals.

"It shouldn't be hard to adapt one of our existing apps to your needs," I murmur, already considering a few viable options. I wouldn't have to make many changes to the interface to get it up and running. "I'm assuming you've established partnerships with the agencies willing to take the referrals for service?"

"Not exactly," Dom says when Killian doesn't speak.

I turn toward my boss. "So the app would need to be easily updated when partnerships are established? That shouldn't be too hard. I've done it before, and I can provide training materials he can use to train his staff on how to add services to the database."

"You misunderstand, Ms. Connor," Killian interjects.

I shift my focus back to him.

"My program provides all services in-house."

"You provide everything?" I blink at him. "Housing? Vocational training? Therapists? Job referrals?"

He jerks his chin in a nod.

"I'm not sure I understand," I admit. Despite the fact that we're situated close to Camp Pendleton, I've never heard of an organization in the area that provides all essential services to vets in need, not including the VA, which is overburdened and underfunded. If his company plans to help fill the gap, he has my full support, but an endeavor like that would be a massive undertaking and take serious funding.

"Killian works with the military," Dom explains when Killian makes no attempt to do so. "He runs a...program"—he hesitates on the word like it's not quite the right one—"that provides reacclimation services to vets returning from overseas. They have on-site housing for up to two-hundred vets, as well as classrooms and medical facilities. They have a team of therapists, doctors, and teachers, as well as support staff in place. The app will simply help them determine what services vets require so they're prepared to meet their needs."

"Oh." I blink again, surprised. "And this is already in place?"

Killian gives another nod. He really doesn't say much.

"The app will streamline the process and ensure everything is set up and ready to go for their vets upon arrival at the facility," Dom continues for him. "The interface needs to be simple and secure, but effective."

"How are vets chosen?"

"Referral," Killian says.

"From whom?"

He eyes me, not speaking.

"That's the tricky part," Dom mutters for him. "We're not allowed to ask any questions about who the vets are or how they're referred to his program."

I frown, not sure I like the sound of that. It seems...exclusive almost. I spent my high school years in a boarding school where exclusivity was the name of the game. I don't regret it, but it wasn't easy to be one of a handful of scholarship students surrounded by the daughters of politicians and celebrities.

"We serve soldiers returning stateside from highly classified assignments," Killian states.

"That I can't know about," I say, understanding dawning. There is a measure of exclusivity, but for good reason. Even if he wanted to tell me about who they serve, he can't because their missions were classified.

He jerks his chin in yet another nod. I'm beginning to think this man communicates primarily through movements of his chin and the narrowing of his eyes. And yet, his presence in the room is almost overwhelming.

I tap my foot against the chair leg, thinking. Even though he makes me nervous, I want to help him. Not just because of my dad, but because of the people out there like him who need to help. I'm guessing those who worked in classified positions probably need it just as badly as anyone else coming home from combat.

"I'll pay you one hundred thousand dollars," Killian says abruptly.

"You mean you'll pay him a hundred thousand dollars," I say, pointing at Dom. He owns the company. I just work here.

The look on Dom's face gives me pause. "He's not here to hire the company," he says. "He's here to hire you."

"Me?" I open my mouth a couple of times, only to snap it closed again. "Why me?"

Neither of them says anything.

"Why me?" I ask again, staring at Killian.

"Why not you?" he says.

I narrow my eyes on him, not buying that non-answer for a minute. No one walks through the doors and demands me personally. And they definitely don't offer me six figures to work on a project for them. I'm good at what I do, but I'm not that good and I'm not that well known, especially with Silicon Valley just a day's drive from here.

"You did some work for my brother last year," Killian says when I say nothing.

"Sebastian," I say, immediately making the connection. Of course. How did I miss it? Sebastian told me he had a twin brother. They aren't identical, but they do look alike now that I'm thinking about it. They're both big and imposing, with stern features and intense eyes. Sebastian's are so dark they're almost black, though.

Killian's jaw clenches like he's irritated, though I don't understand why. Sebastian Thorne is...well, he's not really a friend because I don't have those. But he is someone I admire. His family—Killian's family, I guess—is ridiculously wealthy, and he did a lot for the community before moving to San Francisco a few months ago. I forgot he had a twin brother, though.

"I'll help you," I agree before I can stop myself.

"Because of Sebastian," Killian growls, irritation flaring in his gaze again.

The sight of it there annoys me. I didn't agree because of his twin, but because I can do a lot of good with a hundred grand, and because I *want* to help him help soldiers in need. But why should he care even if Sebastian was my reason? Before I can disabuse him of the notion that I agreed because of his brother, he stands up.

"I'll send the contract to you this afternoon," he mutters. "I expect you to be in first thing in the morning."

"I have other clients," I snap.

He ignores me, turning to Dom. "I need her first thing in the morning."

"We'll work it out," my boss says, the traitor.

Killian gives another of those infuriating nods and then strides toward the door.

I bite my tongue, resisting the urge to tell him to go to hell. Regardless of what he thinks about me and my reasons for agreeing, I still want to help. Too damn bad it means working with his crabby, sexy ass because I already know that's going to go *so* well.

"That went well," Dom says when the door clicks closed behind Killian.

I turn my glare on him, which makes him laugh loudly. "What? It did."

"I'm not talking to you for the rest of the week," I sniff, rising to my feet and adjusting my top. "And I'm telling Summer you're a jerk."

"He likes you."

"Right." I roll my eyes at my boss. If that was Killian liking me, I'd hate to know how he acts toward people he doesn't like. "I guess I have things I need to do this afternoon since I'm reporting for duty first thing in the morning. Are you sure you're okay with this?"

Dom is such a laid-back boss, it's not unusual for engineers to take time off to work on their own projects. Dom says it's good experience that benefits us all in the end. But usually there's a little more lead time involved.

"Yep. The networking project can wait. I don't think Killian can do the same." He grins at me, humor glinting in his emerald eyes.

"I hate you," I mutter, though we both know that's a lie. Dom took a chance on me when no one else wanted to hire a twenty-one-year-old college student with zero actual work experience. I love my job here and he's an incredible boss. Still annoying though.

"Have fun!" His laughter chases me from his office.

I can think of a lot of things working with Killian will probably be...but I don't think fun is among them. He's so...so *ugh*! Why does he have to be so hot and a jerk? And why did he seem so irritated about the fact that I know his brother?

Chapter Two

KILLIAN

"How'd it go?" Sebastian asks as soon as I answer my phone.

"Fine," I growl...though I'm not at all sure that's an accurate assessment of how my meeting with Liberty Connor went. Not only is she intelligent as all hell, she's a knockout, with glossy mink brown hair that's dyed blonde at the tips, bottomless honey-colored eyes, pouty red lips, and a killer body. Her lush curves are a wet dream come true. A rough son of a bitch like me could get lost in a woman like Liberty Connor and not regret a second of it.

Too damn bad she's slept with my brother.

I pace around my office at the reminder, pissed all over again that he got to her before I could. I want her. My dick hasn't gone down since she looked at me with fire in her eyes and her teeth sunk into her pouty bottom lip. Grown men who command troops of their own don't even look at me like she did.

I'm damn good at reading people though, and Liberty is an open book. She may want me to think she's a fierce lioness, but she's a harmless little lamb. I guess it's a good thing Sebastian got to her first. A girl like her needs someone who can be soft and sweet...and that damn sure isn't me. I'm thirty-six, set in my ways. I've spent most of my adult life in the military, grinding the challenge out of even the toughest of men.

I don't date. I don't do love. I'm not that kind of man. It's been years since I've been with anyone. But the filthy shit I want to do to Liberty Connor runs through my head in a loop. I want to see my marks in her skin, see how much she can take before she breaks for me. A big part of me wants to protect her too, keep her safe from whatever put that sadness in her eyes. She tries hard to hide it, but I saw it. And I fucking hate it.

"Fine?" Sebastian chuckles. "So it was that bad, huh?"

"You didn't mention that you'd slept with her," I mutter before I can stop myself. I make another circuit around my office, glaring at the boxes still sitting in the corner, waiting for me to unpack them. I've been stateside for the last six months, but I'm still living out of boxes here and at home.

Sebastian laughs so hard I consider hanging up on him. "You think I slept with Liberty? What the fuck gave you that idea?"

"She likes you." Why do I sound petulant?

"You've spent too much time in the desert," Sebastian says, still laughing. "I've never slept with Liberty. We've never even dated."

Well...shit.

I rub the back of my neck, feeling sheepish and an overwhelming sense of relief. She's not off limits. Fuck. I'm not sure if that's a good thing or a bad thing right now. Even if she hasn't slept with my brother, she's too good for a man like me. My hands are stained with the blood of the men I've killed for my country.

"She's a good girl, Killian," Sebastian says as if reading my mind. "She's different."

"What does that mean?" I growl, not liking the sound of that at fucking all.

"It means she's a friend," he says, his voice firm. "She's not the kind of girl who sleeps around. And despite your opinion of me, I don't either."

"I never said that," I object, pulling the phone away from my ear to glare at it.

"You didn't have to say it," he mutters. "You accused me of sleeping with her like it's something I do regularly. I don't. It's been..." He pauses like he's thinking about it. "Shit. It's been two years since I got laid."

"Jesus." I stare at the phone for a long moment and then expel a heavy breath. How'd I manage to piss both him and Liberty off in the space of a single afternoon? "I don't think about your sex life. She just seemed to like you and I made a wrong assumption."

"You're jealous."

"I'm not fucking jealous," I lie, even though I'm definitely fucking jealous. Which I have never been in my life. But I felt possessive of her the second I set eyes on her. The feeling has only grown in the hours since.

Sebastian snorts. "Whatever you say. My point is, she's had a rough life. She's got up more walls than you do. Even if I had wanted to date her, it never would have happened. I actually admire her, and she's been a big help to me. Don't make me regret referring you to her."

"Fair enough," I mutter, though I really want to demand that he tell me who made her life hard so I can find and eliminate them, and then I want to tell my brother to fuck off for telling me what to do. Which is odd in and of itself. Sebastian and I don't fight. We rarely argue. Growing up, it was the two of us against the world.

We both joined up as soon as we turned eighteen. Sebastian got out years ago, but I liked the order the Marines brought to my life, the routine. There was never much of that growing up. Our father was rarely around, and our mother was too preoccupied with the socialite life to spare much attention to her two young sons. By the time she died and our father remarried, we were teenagers, capable of looking after ourselves.

I've never been jealous of Sebastian. Hell, I've never been jealous period. But Liberty already has me turned inside out and upside down. I shouldn't have demanded that she work here. The demand popped out before I could call it back, though. Simple fact is...I want her in my space, not in Dominic Alessi's. Not in my twin brother's. In *mine*.

I glance around at said space, wondering what she'll think of it. We converted an old hospital to meet our needs. My office isn't fancy, but it's more than big enough for me, the carpet is new, and the paint fresh. A handful of books are aligned neatly on the shelves lining one wall, and stacks of paperwork are ordered just as neatly on the corner of the ornate desk.

A desk I had brought in for Liberty sits off to the side. The rest of the room is full of unpacked boxes and equipment I haven't had time to find a home for just yet. The rest of the place is in a similar state. We hit the ground running as soon as I had boots on the ground, but a project of this magnitude takes time, energy, and a helluva lot of work.

Two wings of the hospital have been converted into housing units for the men, with kitchens and common rooms in each wing. Their bedrooms aren't fancy, but they are private. Soldiers like the ones we'll be serving don't expect fancy anyway. They've been in the most hellish sorts of places, sleeping in conditions not conducive to rest. Here, they'll be able to rest easy while they reacclimate to life, surrounded by men who know exactly what they've been through and what's still ahead. And there is still so much shit ahead for each of them.

None of them will return the same as they were when they left. The things they've seen and done in the name of God and country...well, some memories you can't erase. Quite frankly, I'm tired of watching my men and others like them die because there is no one to watch out for them once they're home, no one to talk to about the classified shit they did to keep our people safe. Even with the new laws that have passed in the last few years, most soldiers like mine don't seek help because they're honor bound by their own oaths to keep quiet about their missions.

This program quashes that dilemma. Everyone here has security clearance. Everyone here has worked classified missions of their own. Everyone here knows what it's like to come home different than they were when they left. It took a miracle and an ungodly amount of money to get it going. But I've got nothing but time on my hands since I'm no longer in active status, and my family has more than enough money to burn. What good is having it if I can't use it to help the people who need it?

"Take care of her," Sebastian orders me, like I'd let anything bad happen to her.

I need her brain, especially if she's as good as he says she is at developing the kind of shit we need here. I want to ensure we've got everything these guys will need ready to go before they ever step foot in this facility. She's going to help me make sure we can do that. I know how to get unruly soldiers in line and get them home safe. I know fuck all about designing programs, coding, or any of the shit Liberty does.

Even if she can't do what I need, I'd still watch out for her. Not that I think she'll let me do it. She did not seem thrilled with me when I left today. Hell, maybe that's for the best. She's got her whole life ahead of her, and I don't have a place in said life.

Even though I know that's true...I already know that's not going to stop me from making her mine.

⁂

Bright and early the next morning, I find myself in the lobby, waiting impatiently for her to arrive. I'm restless and agitated...the same way I have been since I saw her yesterday. I jerked off twice last night to dirty fantasies of her, and then again this morning. My dick is still hard and heavy in my black BDUs, anticipation a tight coil in my stomach.

She's got up enough walls to make Ft. Knox look like child's play, but I'm going to knock them all down, possess her.

No retreat.

No surrender.

I glance around the lobby, curious what she'll think of this place. The seal and emblem for each branch of the military is painted on one cream wall, with a Latin idiom painted beneath. *Pax intrantibus, salus exeuntibus.* Peace to those who enter, health to those who depart. This is a refuge for those who need it, a port in the storm.

I hope she's comfortable here with me. I want it to be a port for her too, a place she can let down her guard and know she's safe. With me, she'll always have that. I just have to find a way to make her want it...to want me.

I don't think she likes me much.

Jesus. Maybe I should have done more than bought her flowers and a blanket for her desk.

The door opens while I'm deliberating, and she steps through, pulling me up short. I lock my legs in place, fighting the urge to go to her. She looks ravishing in a pretty blue top that's tight beneath her tits and then flares out into some sort of pleats. The blue skirt matches her top. Her long legs are bare, a pair of pretty black heels on her feet. Her hair is up in an intricate bun today. Her pouty lips are pink. Her sooty lashes are dark. Her cheeks turn pink when she sees me waiting for her.

"You're late," I growl. My dick is so hard it's painful. I can't think through the wall of lust pounding through me in relentless waves. The things I'm going to teach this girl. Jesus Christ, I should be ashamed of the filthy, kinky shit

I'm going to do to her. I'm not. The coil of anticipation in my stomach winds tighter, cinching my balls up tight.

"It's 7:45," she says, her honey-eyes flashing with annoyance. "You said be here at eight."

Damn. It feels later.

"Come with me," I mutter, turning on my heel. I take a deep breath, trying to get myself under control again. It's impossible. I smell her like she's been all over me. She smells like coconut and sugar, reminding me of the pies our nanny used to make for us. I have a feeling she's going to taste even better than they did.

Her heels click against the floor as she follows behind me. She doesn't speak to me, though I hear her muttering beneath her breath. She's probably calling me a jackass. I don't know how to be soft and sweet like she deserves. It doesn't come natural to me, but I want to try though.

I stop outside the office we're sharing and hold the door open for her.

Her body brushes against mine when she ducks through. I fight back the hungry growl threatening to erupt. Slow. I need to take it slow with her. Give her time to trust me. And then I can fuck her until she's pleading for mercy.

She freezes right over the threshold, going stock still. "We're sharing an office?"

"Don't have an extra one," I lie.

"You didn't say we'd be sharing an office."

"Forgot," I lie again, ducking in behind her. I didn't forget and we don't have to share an office, but we're going to anyway. I want her where I can see her. She's far prettier than any view I've had lately. There is beauty in nature, but that beauty doesn't show up often in the kind of places I've spent the last fifteen years inhabiting.

Her irritation vanishes when she notices the flowers on her desk. She turns to face me, her expression soft. "You got me flowers?"

"And a blanket," I mutter. "I like it cold."

"Thank you," she whispers.

We stare at each other for a long, silent moment before I move toward her, slipping the purse off her shoulder to drop it on her desk. I tip her face up toward me so I can see her clearly. Her eyes are dark beneath even though she tried to hide the shadows with makeup.

"You're tired."

"I didn't sleep well."

"You don't like me."

She blinks at me, caught off guard. "I don't know you enough to dislike you," she says, being honest with me. "You make me nervous."

"Why?"

"You're...different than anyone I know." Her cheeks heat, her gaze slipping away from mine before it comes right back like she can't help herself.

"Different how?"

She shrugs, looking away again. Interesting. She can't face me when she's lying. I file that information away for later.

"Different how?"

"The way you look at me," she says, taking a breath and meeting my gaze again. She holds it, refusing to look away this time. "No one ever looks at me like you do."

"That's because I see you." I hesitate for a brief moment, and then decide to go for broke. I want her to know where this thing between us is headed. She wants me too. Even if she never admits it, I know she wouldn't be here right now if she wasn't interested. "You had my dick hard before you ever opened your mouth."

A pretty blush blooms on her cheeks. She doesn't tell me to go to hell or slap me, so I take that as a good sign.

"You're not so bad yourself," she finally says, looking at me from beneath those long, sooty lashes. "You look like a warrior." She laughs a little. "I guess that's fitting, huh?"

"You like looking at me?"

She rolls her eyes. "I'm sure women are always hitting on you."

"You'd be wrong," I mutter.

She blinks at me, clearly surprised. Which is just fucking cute. The fact that she's attracted to me makes me feel ten feet tall and bullet proof.

"I haven't dated in years."

"Oh." She frowns, her brow crinkling. "Why not?"

"Until six months ago, I was in the desert. Since then? No one has caught my attention." I meet her gaze, holding it. "Not until yesterday."

She blushes again, making my cock leak.

"What about you?"

"I don't date either."

"Not yet you don't," I mutter, releasing her before I do something she'll regret and kiss her. "That'll be changing."

She opens her mouth and then snaps it closed again. I don't miss the little glimmer of hope in her eyes. Nor do I miss the fact that her nipples are hard little points in her pretty blouse.

Jesus, I can't wait to ruin this girl.

Chapter Three

LIBERTY

I STARE AT KILLIAN, not sure what to say to him. My head is spinning. I expected him to be gruff and a little hostile like he was yesterday. Instead he's being...sweet. It obviously doesn't come natural to him, but that makes it somehow even better. The fact that he bought me flowers and a blanket is honestly adorable. No one has ever done anything like that just to make me comfortable.

He looks incredible in his black BDUs and tight white t-shirt. Somehow, he's even more gorgeous than he was yesterday. Or maybe I just convinced myself last night that he wasn't as hot as I remembered. I barely slept all night. I tossed and turned, worried about how today was going to go. So far, it's nothing like I expected.

"I started working on some ideas yesterday," I blurt out.

"Yeah?"

I nod.

He tugs me toward my desk, urging me to sit. "Get comfortable. We have a few minutes before debriefing. You want coffee?"

"Debriefing?"

"Staff meeting," he explains, already headed toward the door. "Coffee?"

"With sugar, please."

He ducks out, leaving me alone in the office. I stare after him, shaking my head. He's intense, someone who clearly prefers to act rather than talk. It's charming in a weird way. He doesn't second guess himself. He just makes a decision and rolls with it.

I pull my phone out and send a quick text to Summer to let her know I made it.

Bestie: Don't kill him. Dominic won't let me visit you in jail. :)

Me: Funny. I'm not going to kill him. He's sweet.

Bestie: We like him now? I thought we didn't like him. When did this change?

Me: He bought me flowers.

Bestie: WHAT?!

Me: Long story. Call you later?

Bestie: You better! Love you. Have fun with your hot Marine. #oohrahoroohlala

I smile like a crazy person when I read her hashtag. God, I love her.

I set my phone to the side and hop up to look around. His office—*our* office, I guess—is large and freakishly neat. Even the stack of files on the corner of his desk are perfectly aligned. Save for the books on the shelf behind his desk and several awards hanging on the wall, there aren't a lot of personal touches. Except for the little vase of wildflowers sitting on my desk. There's also a pink footstool underneath my desk.

His awards catch my eye, so I move behind his desk to get a better look at them. I only recognize one or two of the fifteen hanging in frames on the walls, but I'm not really surprised to see so many of them. He's kind of a badass. It's sexy...though I'm quickly coming to learn that just about everything he does is sexy to me.

I internet stalked him yesterday. Actually, Summer and I internet stalked him yesterday. He's a decorated war hero. He's been in the military since he was eighteen. He got the scar on his cheek saving a family and a group of soldiers from an IED in Afghanistan seven years ago. He could have taken an honorable discharge then, but he didn't. He reenlisted after he healed and then went into IRR status six months ago.

In addition to his twin brother, he also has two younger sisters, Kennedy and Caroline. Aside from that tidbit, there was nothing about his personal life to be found. I guess because he hasn't had much of one for so long. I kind of like knowing that there isn't a long string of women in his past though. I also like knowing he's attracted to me, though I have no idea what to do about that.

Being around him is different. I like the way he looks at me and the way my stomach clenches every time he does it. He's gruff and abrupt, but I don't think he means to be rude. That's just the way he is...I'm guessing because he's been in the military for most of his life.

"You like him," I mutter, refusing to lie to myself about it. I move from his awards to his books. They're all neatly arranged, but in a way that makes my head hurt. Every book is arranged by height, then color, then genre and title. My books are crammed on my shelves based on how often I reread them. He's methodical, precise. And the books he reads are way above my head. He's got everything from books on psychiatry to weaponry. The handful of fiction titles are all classics like *Dante's Inferno* with a couple of science fiction titles thrown in.

I browse through them for another minute or two before looking at his desk. There's a photo on his desk of him and Sebastian, and two younger girls...Caroline and Kennedy, maybe. His sisters are a lot younger than him and Sebastian. Kennedy is tiny, with an innocent face and trusting green eyes. Caroline has red hair and a mischievous smile with dark eyes like Sebastian's. They all share the same sharp cheekbones, full lips, and nose.

"Coffee," Killian says, appearing in the doorway with two paper cups in his hands.

"Are these your sisters?" I ask, nodding at the picture on his desk.

"Yeah," he grunts, stalking toward me.

"Thank you." I take my cup from him and take a sip. It's perfect. "They're a lot younger than you and Sebastian."

"Yeah. Eighteen and twenty-one."

I can tell by the gentleness in his eyes that he has a soft spot for his little sisters. He probably dotes on them. I bet he's overprotective too. I think it's sweet. "They're beautiful."

"I know." He scowls like that fact pisses him off. He's definitely overprotective. I bet he puts their boyfriends through hell. He looks at the picture and then at me again, not speaking.

"Can I ask you a question?"

He nods.

"Did you really receive a Purple Heart for saving a family from an IED?"

"Yes." His gaze shifts across my face. "You looked into me."

"I did," I admit, not trying to lie about it. I'm not a very good liar. "It seemed like the smart thing to do since I'll be working with you for a while."

His lips lift into a tiny smile.

Lord, he's handsome when he smiles.

I take a sip of coffee like that's going to make him less gorgeous.

"You said you started working on some ideas for me," he says.

"Yeah...um, yes." I have to stop to clear my throat. "I already have a basic application we can build on and tweak to fit your needs. It'll collect necessary data on your men in the form of a questionnaire and then compile it into a profile and make suggestions for services based on their responses. Your staff will be able to add their own assessments and update their records through the app as well, sort of like online services and digital charting at a doctor's office."

"Can we keep it secure?"

I nod. "We've used the software before to code a program for a group that provides free medical care to low income families and for a few other data sensitive projects, so it's already AES compliant. Since AES encryption is the standard for classified information, it should pass any required security tests by military officials."

"How long will it take to get it up and running?"

"I need at least a week. And then another to test it out and make any changes."

He arches a brow, clearly surprised. "Two weeks?"

"I work fast, but I don't work miracles," I mumble.

"That's faster than I expected."

"Oh." I take another drink of my coffee. It's surprisingly good. "Like I said, the foundation is already there. It's just a matter of plugging in the specifics and getting all the moving parts working together. I'd also like to add a few features for the men you serve."

"Such as?"

"Even though your program will provide any necessary services, I'd like to add a feature that allows participants to communicate with one another with some level of anonymity. People tend to recover faster when they have the ability to form their own support networks. It'll be like a chat room, accessible only to those in your program."

"They'll be anonymous?"

"If they want to be," I say. "The choice should be theirs to make."

"Agreed."

"You can use it for group sessions as well."

"You're good at this."

I smile at him, proud of myself. I've worked hard to get where I am in life. It's nice to have that recognized without someone attaching a "for a girl" to the end of it. Women in this field still don't get a lot of respect. I can tell by the look in his eyes that he's different though.

We lapse into silence, both sipping our coffee and pretending like we aren't both staring at each other. I can't help but look at him though. His presence is hard to ignore. He commands attention and respect. The way he carries himself is confident and sexy as hell.

"Where'd you learn to do all this?" he asks eventually.

"I taught myself mostly." Computers and programs always fascinated me, so I taught myself how they work. I coded my first program when I was fourteen.

"You went to school for this shit?"

"Sort of."

"Sort of?"

"I haven't finished my degree," I confess, hoping that's not a dealbreaker for him. I could use the money he's offering me for this project to finish paying for school. And even if I don't have a degree yet, I *can* do this for him. "I'm still working on it."

"How old are you?"

"Twenty-two."

He processes that for a moment, a little furrow between his brows. "Why haven't you finished?"

"I can't afford to go full-time," I mumble, glancing down at my cup to avoid seeing the pity in his eyes. His family is the kind of rich you read about in magazines. Literally. There were tons of stories about his family when Summer and I Googled him yesterday, just not much on him specifically. "I'll be finished later this year."

"Not many can work full time and put themselves through school."

"Sometimes, we don't have a choice." Dom pays me well, but I couldn't afford school if I didn't work. Despite having the grades in high school, I wasn't offered much in the way of scholarships. I couldn't afford the application fees and extra testing like a lot of the other girls could and I didn't have anyone to advocate for me.

He doesn't say anything, but I can feel the weight of his gaze. He's always watching me.

"So...um...what should I call you?" I ask, feeling awkward again. I'm used to people staring at me because of my weight, but this is different. He doesn't just see a smart, overweight girl. He sees *me*. No one ever sees me.

"Killian."

"*Colonel* or *sir* seems more appropriate given that you're a decorated war hero," I say, nodding toward the awards displayed on the wall.

He cocks a brow. "Should I call you *baby girl* then? It seems more appropriate given how sweet you are."

I blink at him.

"Shit," he says before I can find a response. He pulls his phone out of his pocket to look at it. "We're late for debriefing." He steps toward me, putting a hand on my lower back. I jump, not used to being touched, but he doesn't move away. "Come on."

I let him lead me from the office, my head spinning all over again.

⁂

"You're hovering," I mutter, glancing up from my computer screen to look at Killian. He's standing right behind me again, watching over my shoulder. He's been doing it all morning. After he introduced me to everyone at the staff meeting, he showed me around. His operation here is honestly impressive.

The fact that he's funding it almost entirely by himself is even more impressive. I found that little tidbit out from Kathy, the receptionist who looks like she'd be more comfortable jumping out of an airplane than manning a desk. Killian may be rough around the edges, but he has a big heart and genuinely seems to care about the men he's trying to help here. It's also pretty clear that he runs a tight ship. Everyone was polite and friendly, but they deferred to him. They all seemed to like and respect him.

He stayed glued to my side all morning, barely letting me out of his sight. He really didn't like when one of the therapists tried to talk to me. He growled at the man, who immediately found somewhere else to be. Killian decided we were going on a solo tour right after that.

Now that we're back in the office, I think he's spent as much time watching me work as he has actually working himself. It's making me nervous. I don't work well under pressure. I need to concentrate, but it's impossible to do that when I feel him standing behind me, watching me. All I can think about is how much I want to lean against him and close my eyes. He smells like the outdoors.

"You know what all that shit says?" he asks.

"Yes."

"It looks like a foreign language."

"It is a foreign language. There are rules and structure to computer languages, just like with any language we speak. This language just doesn't mean a whole lot without the technology behind it," I explain. "If you write it on paper, it does nothing. But if you type it in here, magic happens."

He grunts and then jabs a finger toward the screen. "What does this do?"

I glance at the line of code he's pointing at and smile. "That one autosaves your work so you don't lose it." I've been down that road before. Nothing is quite as devastating as losing several hours' worth of work because you forgot to save it. If the people in his program get frustrated if the app crashes, they might not be willing to expend as much effort into answering the questionnaire the second time around. Autosaving eliminates as much of that risk as possible.

"What about this one?"

"That one determines whether or not I get any work done today," I mutter before I can stop myself. He's covering the line of code with his finger so I don't actually know what it says since I can't see it.

He grunts again and then seems to catch on. "Funny," he says. His gravelly voice says something else. "You like challenging me."

"You're very demanding."

One big hand comes down on my shoulder. "You haven't seen demanding yet, baby girl. I can be a mean son of a bitch when I have to be."

I turn my head and crane my neck to look up at him. His jaw is set, his eyes dark. I think he's trying to warn me, but all he manages to do is turn me on. I think...Lord, help me. I think I like that there's a little bit of the devil in him. It appeals to me on levels I didn't even know existed.

"You aren't mean to me."

"No." He meets my gaze, studying me again. "Doesn't mean I won't be rough when I'm buried nine deep in that cunt, breeding you."

My cheeks heat. So does my body.

"You'd love it."

He might be right about that.

"I wouldn't know," I mumble.

Realization flares in his eyes, followed by satisfaction. "You're a virgin."

I nod, not ashamed of it. I've had more important things to focus on in my life. I haven't held onto my virginity out of some sense of obligation to my future husband or anything like that. I just haven't found anyone who interested me enough to make me want to give it up.

"I'll take it easy on you the first time," he says like the two of us are a done deal. His rough palm cups my cheek, his thumb brushing beneath my eye. "You're beautiful all the time, but I know you're going to be a revelation when you're coming for me."

"Killian," I whisper, though I'm not sure if I'm objecting to the way he's speaking to me or if I'm encouraging him to keep going. He's blunt, but his words don't sound crude. Just honest. Yesterday, I thought he was hiding entire volumes behind his eyes, but I was wrong about that. At least partially. What you see is what you get with him. There is no guessing where you stand. He just tells you outright. But there is still something lurking deep within those eyes, something I recognize. *Loneliness.* I think this man is as starved for affection as I have been.

"You're so goddamn pretty when you're feeling shy," he says, speaking so softly I'm not sure if he's talking to me or just to himself. But then his lips lift into another tiny smile. "Get your magic code done, baby girl. I'll go find us some lunch."

He's striding toward the door before I can say anything. I watch him go, my heart pounding against my ribcage. Part of me wants to gather my things and make a run for it before he sends all my walls tumbling and gets too close.

In my life, there is no permanence. People are temporary. They come and go, and I should be used to that by now because it's been that way since I was little...but it still breaks my heart a little bit every time it happens. Dom and Summer are the only ones who have ever stuck around.

I want Killian to stick around too, with a desperation that's completely foreign to me. But I'm terrified he'll be temporary too. And that makes me feel vulnerable as hell.

He's going to break me...own me. I'm going to let him do it. Because even though getting close to him scares the hell out of me, not getting close scares me even more. I barely even know him, but I know instinctively that I'll regret not getting close to him more than anything. Even if he breaks my heart in the end, I want to know him, and I want him to know me too.

My phone buzzes with an incoming text from a number I don't recognize. As soon as I click on it, I know immediately that it's from him.

Killian: Stop overthinking it, baby girl.

I hesitate for a long moment and then fire off a simple response.

Me: Okay.

When Killian returns with lunch, I'm hard at work on the code, trying to tweak it to his specifications. He sets lunch up at his desk before pulling me out of my chair to eat.

"I need to finish this one line first," I object, but he completely ignores me, leading me to his desk with a hand on my back. "Killian, I need to finish it."

"After you eat."

I glare at him.

"Dom said you forget to eat."

"I do not..." I trail off when he shoots me a look full of authority. "Fine, maybe I forget sometimes, but it's not that big a deal. I'm not starving. Obviously."

His brows wing together. "What does that mean?"

"I'm a big girl, Killian. I'm obviously not missing many meals."

"Big girl? What the fuck?" He scowls at me, looking for all the world like a pissed off devil. "Who the fuck told you that?"

"The mirror? Life? Everyone?" I shrug a shoulder. "I know what I look like. Society doesn't let you forget what you look like when you look like I do." They all assume that you're big because you eat too much or because you're lazy. I stopped caring about their opinions a long time ago, but it doesn't change the fact that I'm curvy. It might not bother me, but it bothers a lot of people who express concern about my health like it's any of their business. I may be overweight, but I'm healthy. I eat well and exercise.

That doesn't stop them from making assumptions.

"They're fucking idiots," Killian growls, getting all up in my personal space. One big hand goes around my waist, yanking me up against him until my body collides with his. He tips my head up with a finger beneath my chin, forcing me to face him. "You're a knockout, Liberty."

Jesus, he's hard everywhere. The bulge in his pants is obvious. So is the fact that his entire body is ripped. A shudder wracks my body, a quiet moan escaping my lips. A forest fire flares to life inside, burning me up.

He studies me for another minute and then presses his lips to mine in a hard kiss, one big hand gripping my ass. "Dreamed about this body all night," he says against my mouth. "You've got me all tied up in knots, baby girl."

My core clenches at his honesty, at the way he grips my ass so possessively, like he knows it belongs to him. "Me too," I whisper, touching my tongue to his bottom lip.

He bites mine in return. I grasp onto his shirt and practically mewl into his mouth.

"Fuck," he rumbles before his hand delves into my hair and he really kisses me. His tongue touches mine, a low groan rumbling against my lips. He kisses me like he can't stop himself, using his hand in my hair to tilt my head the way he wants it.

One kiss, and I know I'm in serious trouble. Every cell in my body screams for relief, pleading for him to touch me like no one ever has before.

"Goddamn, baby girl," he growls, biting my lip hard enough to make it sting. He pushes up against me, the hard ridge of his cock digging into my hip. "That sweet mouth tastes like heaven."

"Killian."

He breaks away from my mouth, leaving a trail of kisses across my cheek. His stubble scratches, but it feels so damn good. It feels even better when he rakes his teeth down the tendon in my neck before moving back up to my ear.

"I'm not good enough for you, but you're mine, Liberty," he says, his tongue touching my earlobe. He releases my head, skimming his hand down my body.

I moan when his fingers touch my bare thigh. And then moan again when he drags my skirt up, his callused fingertips sliding against my bare skin as he goes.

"This is mine now too, baby girl," he breathes in my ear, cupping my sex through my panties. His touch is rough and possessive, but somehow so right at the same time. He grinds his palm against me and then presses a kiss to the pulse beneath my ear. "You going to let me ruin you for anyone else?"

"Yes," I whisper.

"Good." He grinds his palm against me again, touches his mouth to mine once more, and then reluctantly releases me. His eyes smolder with desire. He breathes deeply, like he's trying to catch his breath, or maybe he's trying to smell me. I'm not sure.

I bring my hand up, touching it to my lips. They feel swollen.

"Don't regret it," he orders me.

"I...Okay."

Chapter Four

KILLIAN

I SPEND THE AFTERNOON running around the building, dealing with problems. The plumbing in the showers is backed up. There's a scorpion in one of the rooms in the east wing. And somehow, an order for fifteen industrial sized washers turned into a delivery of thirty stackable washers. They won't last a month around here.

By the time I've got everything sorted, it's already close to six. I'm worried Liberty may have snuck out without waiting for me. And I'm still pissed about the fact that she doesn't know how beautiful she is. People are assholes for making her think that way, for making her doubt herself. She's the prettiest little thing I've ever seen.

Being around her is doing a number on my cock. The hard bastard won't go down. Every time my erection abates, I remember the way she moaned or the feel of her soft body colliding with mine and he perks right back up, desperate for relief. I'm beginning to worry I'm going to end up as one of those cautionary tales about what happens when an erection lasts longer than four hours.

I practically run back to our office, only to exhale in relief when I find her behind her desk, squinting at her computer. Her pretty bun is long gone. So are her shoes. She's got her hair pulled back into a simple ponytail with her feet propped up on the footstool I bought her.

"Hey," she says, looking up at me through tired eyes.

Has she taken a break at all since I left after lunch? It doesn't look like it.

"You done yet?" I ask, prowling toward her.

She furrows her brows like she doesn't know what I'm talking about. She's been so caught up in her work, she doesn't even know what time it is. Irritation floods through me. Not with her, but with myself. I should have realized she'd get lost. Alessi tried to warn me that she does it, said she gets so hyper-focused the world could end and she wouldn't even realize it.

I'll take better care of her tomorrow.

"Come on," I murmur, stopping beside her and holding out a hand. "You're done for the day."

"I need to finish this last bit of code," she says, stubborn as hell.

"No."

"Killian."

"No, Liberty."

She narrows her eyes on me.

"You work for me now," I remind her. "I decide when enough is enough. You can't win a war in a day, baby girl."

"I thought we were trying to help them recover from war," she mutters, rolling her eyes at me.

If she were a recruit, I'd be making her sweat for that shit. Lucky for her, I know enough about women to know I can't treat her like she's enlisted, not if I want her to fall in love with me. Instead, I turn her chair around and wrap my hands around her waist, picking her up.

"Killian, put me down!"

I sit her on the edge of her desk. "You're not used to being cared for," I murmur, pressing my lips to her temple. "You'll learn."

"Learn what?" she says, scowling at me when I grab her purse and phone before handing them over to her.

"That I make the rules now. When you obey, you get rewarded. When you don't, you get punished. You'll enjoy it either way." I fish her heels out from under the desk, turning them around in my hands. No wonder women are forever kicking off their shoes. There's no way there's enough space in these things for their delicate toes.

"I'm a big girl."

A growl erupts from my lips.

"I mean, I can take care of myself," she says, rolling her eyes at me again. "Jeez. You're a caveman."

When it comes to her, she's probably right. I want to be the man she leans on, the one who takes care of her, the only one who gets to be intimate with her. I want to be the one she trusts with every piece of herself. The one who gets to take care of her like the treasure she is.

Christ, if my men could see me now, they wouldn't even recognize me. I've always been a hard-ass, more than willing to hand out an ass chewing or launch an attack on our enemies. I'm still more than capable of doing both, but she has some long dormant instinct bubbling to the surface. The one that says she's mine to protect and provide for. The one that wants to alternately fuck her raw and spoil her rotten.

"Never said you couldn't," I mutter, slipping her shoes on her feet. Her little toenails are painted a sparkly purple color. She has a mole on her ankle. I run my hand up her leg before curving it around her hip and tugging her closer to me. "You've been doing it for a long time, baby girl. Now I'm going to be the lucky motherfucker who gets to do it for you."

"Killian," she whispers, her irritation vanishing. Her expression softens, melting like butter.

"You want me to cook for you or do you want to go out?"

"We can go out." She hesitates. "Unless you don't want to."

One day, this infuriating, beautiful woman is going to know beyond a shadow of a doubt that I'd go anywhere so long as I was with her. Getting to spend time with her and show her off is not a hardship. Fuck everyone who ever made her think it was.

The Italian restaurant is packed by the time we get there. The hostess takes my name and promises they'll have a table for us in fifteen minutes. I take advantage of the time and pull Liberty into a corner before wrapping my arms around her. She's tense at first, but within moments, she relaxes and lays her head against my chest, letting me hold her.

A few people shoot us curious glances, but most are too wrapped up in their own conversations to wonder how a scarred son of a bitch like me got lucky enough to be with a goddess like her. She feels so soft in my arms. I instantly become addicted to cuddling her. Which is surprising. I've never been one to cuddle.

Affection wasn't normal in our household. Our parents were too busy with their own lives to spare me and Sebastian much attention. It was our nanny who comforted us when we were sick or afraid, who kissed us on the cheeks and sent us off to school. She died of a heart attack twenty years ago. I don't think I've been held since then.

Holding Liberty is nice though...better than that. It feels a little like coming home.

I hope like hell she feels it too.

Eventually, the hostess motions for me, silently letting us know our table is ready. I reluctantly release Liberty, only to put my hand on the small of her back to guide her. Touching her is quickly becoming my favorite thing to do.

"This way," the hostess mutters, casting furtive glances in my direction, a mix of pity and curiosity on her face. She leads us through the restaurant toward the back, sneaking looks at me every couple of seconds.

People have been staring at my scar for years. It doesn't bother me anymore, but Liberty doesn't seem to appreciate her looking at me like she is.

"It's rude to stare," she tells the girl, her voice firm.

"I'm...so sorry." The girl blushes bright red.

"He's a decorated war hero," Liberty says, still bristling on my behalf. And fuck if that doesn't turn me on like nothing ever has before. The fact that she comes up to my chest but thinks she needs to stand up for me is sexy on levels I can't even begin to comprehend.

One way or another, I'm going to make her fall in love with me.

I know I'm already there with her. Why else does my heart feel like it wants to crawl up my throat and take up residence inside her? It belongs to her now. So do I. If she doesn't come home with me tonight, I'm going to be a miserable bastard.

Neither of us speaks again until we're seated at the back of the restaurant. Our table is situated behind a low retaining wall, offering privacy from the main dining room. We're close enough to the bay to see the lights of the city reflecting off the water in the distance.

"Do people always stare at you like that?" Liberty asks once our waiter brings out a basket of bread and glasses of ice water before disappearing again.

"Usually."

"That's rude."

"Used to it, baby girl." I offer her the basket of bread, waiting until she takes a piece before I grab my own. Her cheeks are pink, though I don't know if it's because she's angry on my behalf or because she's feeling shy again.

"It's still rude."

She's not wrong.

I watch her nibble on her bread.

"You grow up around here?" I ask, curious as hell about her. She knows a lot about me, but she hasn't shared much in return. All I have are the little tidbits I've been able to piece together on my own. I don't like not knowing everything about her. Ordinarily, I'd just call up a buddy and tell him to get me everything there is to know about her...but I don't want to do that. I want her to trust me with the pieces of herself she keeps hidden behind those walls.

She flinches and then shakes her head. "I grew up in Los Angeles. Um...in foster care."

"Your parents are gone?"

She nods, staring at her water like it holds the answers to the universe. "Yeah. My dad was in the military. My mom died while he was overseas. Aneurysm. He didn't handle losing her and his PTSD well and got hooked on drugs. Um, he lost custody of me when I was six." She looks so fucking sad. "He overdosed a little over a year later."

Shit. No kid should have to lose both their parents so fucking young. I don't know why she wasn't ever adopted, but it kills me a little bit to know just how long she's been alone, trying to hold it all together. I'm also proud as hell of her. She's made a life for herself despite everything.

I feel like an ass for thinking she accepted this job because of Sebastian. She did it for her dad, so no other little kid had to lose a parent to the wounds war leaves behind like she did. She's been through hell in her life, but she's still standing. She's got a warrior's spirit.

"I'm sorry, baby girl."

"It was a long time ago," she says like that means it should hurt less. Some wounds don't ever heal, though. They just scab, breaking open over and over again.

"You have any other family?"

She shakes her head, confirming what I already knew.

"I think Sebastian and Alessi would tell me something different," I murmur, resting my elbows on the table and then tenting my hands together to rest my chin on them.

She looks up at me, confusion on her face.

"They may not be blood, but they consider you family." They're both protective of her. I don't like it because she isn't theirs to protect, but I get why. She's the kind of girl you can't help but want to watch over. I'm guessing that's why Alessi hired her so young. I'm also guessing she doesn't realize he watches out for her like an older brother. He put me through the third degree before agreeing to let me meet with her yesterday.

"They're just nice," she says.

"To you. They both threatened me with bodily harm if I hurt you."

The doubt in her eyes is obvious.

My lips kick up in a rueful grin. "Sebastian wasn't thrilled when I accused him of sleeping with you."

Her nose wrinkles. "I've never slept with Sebastian."

"Know that now. Didn't know it yesterday." I hesitate and then admit the truth. "I was jealous as hell he got to you before I could make you mine."

She looks at me like I'm some foreign species, speaking a language she doesn't understand. It's both adorable as hell and frustrating as fuck that she doesn't realize how goddamn perfect she is. That she doesn't know men fight wars over women like her. As much as I like to think I would have walked away and let Sebastian have her had they slept together...my gut says differently.

"Sebastian's just a..."—she hesitates like she isn't sure what he is and then settles on a descriptor—"nice guy. I barely even know him. He barely knows me."

"He knows you better than you think, baby girl."

She opens her mouth to respond and then snaps it closed when our waiter appears.

I barely look at him or the menu, instead watching Liberty. She doesn't look at me, but I know she senses me watching her. Her cheeks are pink and she's jumpy again.

"Um, I'll have the chicken Florentine and a glass of Pinot, please," she says, holding out her menu for the waiter, a young kid with a gap between his front teeth and acne.

"I'll have the Caprese stuffed chicken." I hand my menu over to the kid too. "And a bottle of the Yuengling Gold."

Liberty's nose wrinkles like she finds my choice gross. Guess she's not a beer girl. I'll have to teach her how different good beer can taste.

"I'll have it right out," the kid says, grinning at her. Or grinning at her tits, rather.

"Her eyes are up higher," I snap at him.

He jumps like a young recruit caught acting up.

Liberty flushes bright red. Fuck. I didn't mean to embarrass her.

"Sorry," the kid mumbles before hurrying off. Little prick.

"Thanks," Liberty says before I can apologize for embarrassing her.

"That happen a lot?"

She shrugs, which is answer enough. Her tits are incredible. I'm guessing assholes are always staring at them, imagining what it'd be like to have their hands on them. God knows, I've thought about it a time or ten. I want to leave my marks all over them.

"What do you do when you aren't working, baby girl?" I ask, shifting the conversation back to solid ground. If I don't, we're not going to make it through dinner before I'm all over her. Sitting across from her without being able to touch her is pure hell.

"I mostly read or watch Netflix. Sometimes, I hike or go out for drinks with Summer."

"Summer?"

"Dom's wife." She smiles, her whole face lighting up. "They're so cute together. They just found out she's pregnant, so he spends all his time chasing her around the office, trying to boss her around. She never lets him do it, though."

The image of her pregnant with my baby slams into me, stiffening my cock. It hits me right in the solar plexus, knocking me on my proverbial ass. Jesus, I want to see her belly round with my baby, see her cuddling him or her close.

I take a deep breath, fighting through the crippling ache in my balls. "You like Summer?"

"She's my best friend," she says, still smiling. "I love working with her."

Well, shit. I guess I will have to let her go back to work at some point, then. There's no way I can keep her from her friend, especially when she lights my girl up like fireworks. Maybe I can convince Alessi to let her work partially at my office and partially at his. I make a note to look into it later.

Right now, I have more pressing shit to deal with. Like convincing her to come home with me so I actually manage to sleep tonight.

Chapter Five

LIBERTY

"**Y**OU DON'T HAVE TO walk me to my car," I murmur to Killian, watching him out of the corner of my eye as we stroll through the parking lot, headed toward my Prius. Dinner was...interesting. He can be charming, but I don't think it's something that comes natural to him.

I think it's sweet that he tried for me though.

"Going to anyway," he says, putting his hand on my lower back.

I fight the urge to shiver at the weight of his hand. His longer fingers curve around my hip and squeeze, making my entire body hum with energy. My legs literally shake beneath me.

We walk in silence through the parking lot. The sun is slowly sinking behind the horizon, shadows creeping in to take its place. The parking lot has cleared out since we got here. We didn't talk very much over dinner—I don't think he says much as a general rule—but we both lingered like neither of us wanted to leave. I'm not even sure if this was a date, but I wanted to stay right where I was at, staring at him like a crazy person.

He did a lot of staring of his own. Every time I looked up, his eyes were on me. He didn't even act embarrassed to be caught staring. His lips just kicked up into one of those signature tiny smiles and he kept on doing it. I liked it.

I squeak when we step between two trucks and he grabs me around the waist. My back hits the side of the truck to the right, his hand cupping my head to keep me from cracking it against the window.

His big body presses into mine. His face looms into view, his crystalline eyes on fire.

"Killian, wha–?"

His mouth crashes down on mine, stealing my question and my breath.

My hands fly to his shoulders, a surprised gasp leaving my lips. He grabs my hands in his free hand, pushing them up over my head...holding me captive against the cool metal of the truck behind me. The dominant move liquefies my insides, turning me into a puddle of desire. My entire body trembles, shaking with the force of my need for this man.

He places a sweet kiss to the corner of my mouth and then yanks my skirt up, cupping my center like he did in his office. Only this time, he presses against my clit, sending a powerful jolt through me. "Gotta see you coming before I lose my fucking mind. You going to let me? Right here, right now?"

I nod, not trusting myself to speak. I should probably tell him no. We're in the middle of a parking lot in San Diego and it's not even completely dark out yet. Anyone could walk by and see what he's doing to me. But I don't want to tell him no. Not even a little bit.

His lips kick up into another of those tiny smiles he gives me. He presses a kiss to the corner of my mouth and then to my temple. His hand dips into my panties. "Jesus Christ," he groans. "You're soaked."

I know I am. I think I've been that way since I saw him sitting in Dom's office yesterday morning. I've *definitely* been that way since he kissed me this morning.

He parts my folds, pressing his thumb to my clit.

A jolt of electricity zips through me. I bite my lip hard to keep from crying out his name as he urges me to part my legs a little wider. He touches me like he knows exactly what I need, exactly how to make me come undone for him.

Within seconds, I'm on the edge.

"Can't wait to feel you wrapped around my cock," he says, using his whole hand to get me off. It's dirty and public and yet...I love every single thing about it.

"Killian," I whimper.

"Don't let anyone hear you," he warns me. "Those sounds are just for me."

"I can't be quiet."

"You can."

He's wrong. He is so, so wrong...

The orgasm hits me, heat flowing through me. I bite my lip to keep from crying out his name as it engulfs me, flinging me skyward. My legs tremble, threatening to buckle beneath me. He holds me up against the truck with his body, his mouth slashing down on mine to steal my cries.

I come harder than I ever have before. It seems to go on forever, leaving me gasping and shaking in his arms. When it's over, he cuddles me up against his chest, holding me like I'm something precious.

No one has ever held me like this before, like they didn't want to let me go. Tears sting at my eyes and squeeze my throat in a vise. I don't want it to end. I want to stay right here, soaking up the heat of his body until I'm old and gray.

"Come home with me," he says...though it's more of an order than a request.

I hesitate, torn between giving in and letting him consume me, and protecting myself and my heart. I could easily fall for him. I'm pretty sure I'm *already* falling for him. That scares me and excites me at the same time. But he told me today not to overthink it. So I'm going to take his advice. I'm not going to overthink. I'm going to enjoy whatever time we have together.

I take a breath...and I take a leap.

"I'll go home with you."

Killian wants me to ride with him, but I convince him to let me take my car home instead of leaving it in the parking lot. He doesn't like it but agrees when I remind him that I either need to get clothes now or I'll have to go home to get ready for work in the morning.

By the time we arrive at my condo, I'm a mess of nerves. I know what going home with him signifies...what it means. I'm a little worried I won't live up to the way he's built me up in his mind. To him, I'm a goddess. I feel more like an imposter though.

He's older, hotter, a literal millionaire. He could have anyone or anything he wanted. It's crazy to me that he wants me as badly as I want him...that he *could* want me as badly as I want him. He's the sun, blotting out everything else. And I'm just me. A twenty-two-year-old virgin with abandonment issues.

"You're overthinking it," he says, reading me like a book as soon as he opens my car door and helps me out. He gets in my space again, pulling my body flush against his. His hand skims down my back, gripping onto my ass. His lips seek mine in the darkness, his stubble scraping my chin. "Stop thinking."

He makes that sound so easy.

"I'm nervous," I whisper against his lips. "I've never..."

"Done this before?"

"Wanted anyone this badly."

"Jesus." He bites my lip, using his grip on my ass to pull me closer. "Me neither, baby girl. Need to get my cock in you so fucking bad it hurts. Need to make you fall for me."

"What if you change your mind?"

He growls. Faster than I can process, I'm caught between his body and the side of my car, held captive by his massive frame. He blocks me in with his hands on either side of my head. His crystalline eyes shoot off sparks when they meet mine.

He eyes me for a long, silent minute, looking like a pissed off avenging angel. "I've spent my life looking death in the face, Liberty. I don't have regrets, especially not about you."

"That's not what I meant."

"I know what you meant. You're afraid to let me in."

I nod, unable to deny it.

He expels a heavy breath and then pulls me into his arms. "You don't have to be afraid with me, baby girl. You don't have to keep those walls up either. I'm not going to hurt you."

No, but he might break me. I don't say that though. Instead, I let him hold me.

"Going to teach you what it means to have someone to lean on."

"I've never had that."

"You do now." He kisses me again and then pulls me away from my car, holding my hand like we're two lovers out for a stroll instead of...whatever we are. I'm not even sure at this point. I just know that I don't want whatever this is to end because he's already claimed a big piece of my heart.

"You live here alone?" he asks, guiding me up the steps toward my condo.

"Yeah."

He grunts. I love when he makes that sound. He communicates so much in the simple sound, more than I ever knew anyone could communicate with a grunt. It's way hotter than it should be.

My hands shake a little when I unlock the door. He pushes it open, motioning for me to go in first. The alarm beeps a warning, so I quickly hit the lights and then disarm the system.

Killian follows me inside, looking around. My place isn't fancy. Honestly, it's barely big enough for me, but it's mine. The living room and small kitchen are open, with my bedroom and bathroom down a short hall. The stackable washer and dryer sit beside the fridge, which isn't ideal. But my furniture is new. The deep purple accents look good against the cream walls and hardwood floors.

I glance at him to see what he thinks, but he's staring at me again, his eyes dark with need. My body responds to that look on his face, desire blasting through me in a powerful wave. One second, I'm nervous. The next, I'm pretty sure I'm going to die if he doesn't kiss me again immediately.

"Killian," I whisper, swaying on my feet.

"Fuck." He grabs me by the hips, yanking me into him again. Somehow, he turns us so my back hits the door as his mouth crashes down on mine. A needy growl vibrates in his chest, the sound full of hunger.

It touches me everywhere, coaxing a moan from deep inside. I clutch him to me, tugging at his shirt because I need to feel his skin against mine right now or I might burst into tiny pieces. He seems to know how I feel. He helps me rip his shirt off over his head, his lips leaving mine for only a split second before he's back again, licking inside my mouth and grinding me against his erection.

I run my hands up and down his chest, trying to touch him everywhere at once. His body is literal perfection, made of smooth, contoured muscle and coarse hair. His chest and shoulders are covered in tattoos. He's all man, powerful and strong. And so damn beautiful. I rake my nails down his chest and abdomen, yank at the button on his pants.

He grabs my hands before I manage to get it undone, trapping them against the door above my head. His mouth breaks from mine, leaving a line of kisses down my throat. Before I can protest the fact that he's not letting me touch him, he bites my nipple through my shirt. A shock of pleasure races through me, my legs threatening to give out.

"Goddamn, I can't wait to get my mouth on these," he growls, letting me go to pull my shirt up. Within seconds, he's tossing it over his shoulder, leaving me in nothing but my bra and skirt. His gaze rakes over me, hot and hungry.

I instinctively move to cover my stomach, trying to hide my flaws and imperfections from him.

"No," he says, grabbing my hands before I can do it. He pulls them up over my head again, holding me hostage once more. "Those curves you try so hard to hide? Those are my playground, my temple. I worship them, Liberty." He places the sweetest kiss to the corner of my mouth. "Gonna teach you how beautiful you are, baby girl. You'll never doubt it again."

"Killian." I melt all over again. For someone who doesn't say much, he sure knows all the right words. I love it so much. "I'm not self-conscious usually. Just...no one ever sees me, you know? They look through me or around me. Not you."

"Never me." He presses his lips to mine and then pulls away. "You going to be a good girl and do what I say, or do I need to tie you up?"

Oh. My.

My legs shoot together, my core clenching so hard at the thought that I think I orgasm a little bit. Excitement races through me, adrenaline sending my heart rate spiking. The thought of being completely at his mercy is overwhelming. I want it. Bad.

He notices my reaction. Pure wickedness flares in his eyes, and his upper lip curves into a smile that I already know I'll never tire of seeing on his handsome face. He looks like a warlord, ready to claim his spoils.

"Maybe not an innocent little lamb after all," he says. "You got a little bit of a devilish side, don't you?" He leans in and nips at my shoulder.

"M-maybe," I whisper, my chest heaving up and then down as I try to suck in a breath that doesn't want to come. Lord, he's already got me sweating and overheated and he hasn't even really touched me yet.

"Baby girl, I'm going to do more than make you sweat. I'm going to make you beg," he growls against my skin, letting me know I said that out loud.

I whimper his name, desire boiling low in my stomach. Oh, God. I'm not going to survive this. He's going to ruin me, just like he threatened to do earlier.

He kisses a trail down my chest, groaning long and loud. He buries his face in my cleavage, peppering every inch with kisses and little bites that have me gasping out loud and struggling against the way he's holding my hands hostage. His teeth close around my nipple.

"Killian!"

He adjusts his hold on me, capturing both hands in one of his. He uses the other to undo the clasp of my bra, growling in frustration when it doesn't easily come undone. He tongues my nipple through the lacy fabric and then bites down again. Finally, the stupid clasp releases.

He releases my hands long enough to help pull the straps off my arms. I try to use that momentary reprieve to my advantage and get my hands on him again, but he's a lot faster than I am. He has my arms pinned above my head again in two seconds.

"Fucking hell," he swears, pinching my nipple hard enough to have me sobbing his name, desperate for relief.

My clit pulses in time, another flood of arousal drenching my panties. I chafe my thighs together, trying to find a position that relieves a little of the ache, but it's useless. I'm not even tied up and I'm completely at his mercy.

He replaces his thumb with his teeth, closing them around my nipple. A growl rumbles in his chest, sounding for all the world like a territorial wolf. He licks and sucks and bites until I'm writhing against the door.

"Please, please," I plead, not sure how much more of this delicious torment I can take. It's too much and not enough.

"You need to come, baby girl?"

"Yes!" I sob.

As soon as the word leaves my lips, he releases my hands, dropping to his knees in front of me. I grasp onto his shoulders to hold myself upright because without him helping me, my legs are trembling too hard to do it myself.

"Spent a lot of time in the desert, wondering what heaven would feel like," he mutters, leaning forward to nip at my stomach. "Didn't think it'd be this goddamn perfect, Liberty. Lift your foot." He taps my right calf.

I do as instructed, lifting my foot from the floor for him. He pulls my shoe off, bringing my foot up to press a kiss to the top of it before he places it back on the floor and then repeats the process with my left.

"One day soon, you're going to dig those pretty heels into my back while I'm fucking you," he says, grasping my hips and pulling me forward just far enough for him to reach the zipper on my skirt. The teeth part slowly.

His eyes meet mine, so blue I get a little lost in them.

He tugs my skirt down, allowing it to puddle at my feet. Even then, he holds my gaze captive, seemingly staring into me with adoration blazing in his eyes. Somehow, all those raw, exposed wounds that have always bled a little start to close up, as if he's stitching them back together with nothing more than the conviction in his eyes and the heat of his hands on my body.

"Killian," I whisper, the need to say...something...overwhelming me. But I don't know what to say or how to tell him that I'm falling in love with him.

He breaks my gaze finally, raking his eyes down my body. His chest shudders with the force of his exhale. "Jesus Christ," he breathes, reaching down to squeeze his cock. "You're going to have me coming all over myself like a teenager when I get those pretty panties off, baby girl."

"Do it."

"No. The next time I come, it'll be in that virgin cunt." He hooks his index fingers into my panties and starts tugging them down. "You smell like heaven. Bet your pussy tastes like it too. I'm going to find out."

I grasp the doorknob, trying to keep myself upright.

"Fuck me," he groans, his eyes locked on my pussy like he can't look away. My panties hit the floor, pooling at my feet with my skirt. He leans forward and inhales before groaning again. One big hand latches around my thigh, helping me lift and drape it over his shoulder.

He turns his head, kissing my inner thigh and leaving me trembling all over again. He sinks his teeth into me, biting just hard enough to make me cry out his name. When he pulls back, I see the red mark he left on me. I see the possessiveness lighting his eyes too, feel it pouring over me, drowning me in the deluge of desire left behind.

The first touch of his tongue to my center has me sobbing his name. The second sets my blood on fire. I've never felt such pure, powerful bliss before, as if he's delivering an overdose of it directly into my veins with each decadent, heavenly touch of his tongue.

He grips me hard, pulling me closer, until both of my legs are thrown over his shoulders. His possessive hold on my ass is the only thing keeping me from hitting the floor. He growls my name, using his entire face to get me off. There's nothing slow and sweet about it. Nothing gentle. He's a beast, taking what's his to claim.

And my God, I never want it to end.

I clutch at his hair, grinding shamelessly against his face. I can't stop myself. Something else is in control now, the part of me he woke up yesterday. The one that wants to be naughty and defiant and live for challenging and rattling this man. It grows bigger, brighter inside me as he eats me, groaning my name and kneading my ass in his rough hands.

My heart thunders in my chest like a war drum. Sweat breaks out on my skin. He thrusts his tongue into me, fucking me with it. He's not gentle there either, snarling against my pussy as he fights to get it inside me, to claim that part of me too.

He spreads my cheeks apart, rocking me against his face. His nose grinds against my clit. His stubble abrades the sensitive skin on the insides of my thighs. If this is what heaven feels like, I never want to leave.

"Killian!" I shout, surprised when I feel his tongue against my back entrance. It feels good, better than I ever imagined that would feel. He presses against the tight ring of muscle, jostling his tongue back and forth until I'm sobbing his name so loud my throat hurts.

"Goddamn," he growls, pushing away from the door with his hands.

I cry out, afraid I'm going to fall, but he holds me like it's easy, moving us until I'm sprawled out on the cool hardwood. He spreads my thighs wide, holding them down. His tongue swipes through my folds again, striking against my clit with startling precision. I grow wetter, wilder, more desperate. The cold wood at my back does nothing to cool me down. There is an inferno raging inside me, growing bigger by the minute.

I've touched myself before, but I already know what's coming is more massive than anything I've ever felt. It's going to destroy me, leave me in broken, jagged little pieces. I guess it's a good thing I'm already on the floor.

He seams his lips around my clit, pushing one finger inside me, and then another. He fucks me with them hard, not letting up. He's relentless, implacable. God, he's a machine.

I scream his name, bursting apart at the seams. My climax hits hard, blinding me with pleasure. I sob, writhing my way through it. I lose myself in it and the overwhelming peace it sends careening through me. Everything falls away except the pleasure. And there is so much of it. My God. He really is ruining me.

I love it.

When I come back to myself, Killian's on his knees between my thighs, naked. His cock is long and thick, the head almost purple. He's so much bigger than I'm prepared for. Jesus, he's going to split me down the middle with that thing. I want him to do it. So badly I tremble beneath him.

"Killian," I whisper.

"Fucking perfect," he grunts, leaning forward to kiss my belly and then nip at my waist. He shoves his hands under my ass, yanking me toward him. My legs fall open wider, giving him more room between them. His jaw is clenched tight, stark hunger stamped across every line of his face as he stares at my wet sex.

He lines himself up at my entrance, dragging his gaze up to mine. "Can't wait, baby girl," he grits out between his teeth. His chest shudders up and down, his breath a harsh pant. He's discomposed, undone. More beautiful than anything.

"Don't wait," I whisper back, reaching out for him. "I need you to make me yours, Killian."

"You're already mine."

He's right. He has no idea how right he is.

"It's going to hurt," he mutters. "Don't know if I can be gentle."

I don't think I want it gentle. He told me he likes it rough...I want to see him like that, want to feel how rough he can get. I already know having him inside me is going to knock my world out of orbit, completely change the trajectory of my life.

"I don't want gentle."

A little bit of the devil peeks out from his eyes again. He grabs my hands in his, holding me still beneath him...and then he thrusts into me hard. My body resists the intrusion for a moment before finally letting him in. At first, I feel pressure, and then he thrusts deeper.

A sharp bite of pain rips through me as my virginity gives way, shredding. It hurts like hell. Tears sting at the backs of my eyes as the pain worms its way through me. I try to wriggle away from it, to make it hurt less, but he has me locked in place, refusing to let me go. I fight him, but it gets me nowhere. He's an implacable wall of muscle.

"Breathe, Liberty," he growls, his gruff voice cutting through the fog of pain. "You can take it, baby girl. Breathe."

I suck in a deep breath and then another, expel them on a sob.

"Good girl," he says.

My inner muscles clench around him at his praise. The pain slowly starts to dim and fade. Killian watches me like always, assessing, studying...reading me like I'm his favorite book. I think he's trying to stay still, but he keeps moving, pushing deeper before easing back a little, like he can't stop himself. His muscles are all locked up tight, practically bulging with the effort he's expending.

Knowing that he's this worked up, that being inside me has him fighting for control is a powerful feeling. I clench around him. His lip curls back, a growl leaving his lips. He pulses his hips again, pushing deeper, until he's fully seated in me.

I feel him everywhere.

"So fucking tight," he groans. "Goddamn, baby girl. You're my new favorite toy."

Pleasure slowly creeps in, taking place of the pain. He feels massive inside of me, stretching me. I'm so full. And he looks like a God above me, so powerful and fierce.

He releases my hands to yank me up onto his thighs.

"Going to fuck you now," he warns me.

"Yes."

The plea barely leaves my lip before he's moving, raging like a storm against me. He grips my ass, using it to yank me down onto him and then push me off. I cry out, shocked at how good it feels, at how incredible he looks with his muscles all working together. His jaw is clenched tight again, his lips curled back from his teeth.

He takes me hard, fucking me so deep it knocks the breath out of me over and over. He falls forward, catching himself on his forearms. His teeth latch around my nipple, biting hard enough to have me clawing down his back.

He seems to like that.

"Mark me," he growls, releasing my nipple to drag his teeth down the tendon in my neck. "Let everyone see what a dirty little virgin you are, Liberty. Let them know that I popped your cherry and you fucking loved it."

Jesus, his mouth. The filthy things he's saying have me writhing beneath him. Every thrust grinds his pelvis against my clit, sending me spiraling toward another orgasm.

"Jesus Christ. I'm never leaving this cunt," he swears, biting my neck and then moving to my mouth to bite my lip. He thrusts his tongue inside my mouth like he's fucking me there too, like he needs to have as much of himself inside me as possible. "I'm going to have you on your back, begging for my cock at every opportunity."

"Please," I plead, more than willing to give him that if it means letting him make me feel like this.

He yanks my thigh up over his hip, changing the angle. He pounds into me, relentless, ruthless. My back inches across the hardwood, my hair getting caught in small imperfections in the wood. The way it pulls drives me higher, makes me plead louder.

"I'm your God now, baby girl," he says on a wicked thrust. "This pussy belongs to me."

"Yes!" I scream, clawing down his back again and writhing as he strikes some magical spot inside that has me seeing stars. He seems to know what he's found because his eyes light up, and he does it again and again, cursing and snarling like a beast every time he hits that spot, and my walls clamp around him.

"Going to fuck a baby into you," he says in my ear before biting my lobe.

I cry out at his words, the coil in my belly winding up tight at the thought.

He slips one hand between us, sliding his fingers through my sticky folds before moving it lower. He touches my back entrance, pressing against the tight ring of muscle like he did with his tongue. Only he doesn't stop this time. He pushes until his thumb slips into me.

I moan at the foreign sensation, stunned all over again by how good it feels to be touched there. He seems to know how much I like it. He groans my name, pushing that finger in and out of me, toying with me until I'm on the edge, overwhelmed with pleasure.

"You want to come?" His gritty voice rakes across my senses.

"Yes, please, Killian," I plead, not above begging. Need claws through me so fiercely it's almost painful. I need to come or I'm going to explode into tiny pieces. There won't be any putting me back together again if I do. I already know it. The pressure is too much, too powerful.

"Come on my cock, and make me a daddy." He pumps his hips, fucking me hard. His hand is caught between us, his thumb moving in and out of me. The dual sensations and his dirty words are my undoing.

My legs lock around his waist, my back bowing off the floor as the orgasm hits me. I cry out over and over, sobbing as the pressure detonates deep inside and ripples outward, submerging me in choppy waves. My pussy grows wetter as I drown in the pleasure, my nails in his skin and his name on my lips.

He roars my name into the room, thrusting into me hard enough to steal my breath as my orgasm pulls his own from him. I feel his cock jerking as he comes inside me, feel the heat of his release spreading through me, coating me in him.

Knowing there's nothing to stop him from getting me pregnant sets off a tidal wave of aftershocks. They swarm through me one after the other. I thrash and cry out, trying to pull him closer, to keep him as deep inside me as possible.

He seems more than content to stay there.

"Liberty," he groans in my ear. "Jesus Christ, you're strangling my cock." He circles his hips, grinding against my clit, working every last bit of pleasure out of my pliant body as he can. He's greedy for it, determined to claim me all the way down to my soul.

And then he steals even that, possessing me thoroughly with three whispered words.

"I love you."

Chapter Six

KILLIAN

LIBERTY AND I DON'T make it to my house. We barely make it off the living room floor, but I know she can't possibly be comfortable after I fucked her like a beast. I feel a little guilty about that. She was a virgin and I took her hard. I know she got off on it though. I also know she heard what I said...but she didn't say it back.

She's quiet as I pick her up, carrying her down the short hall to her bathroom. I turn the shower on and let it heat while I cuddle her against my chest. Neither of us speaks, but it's a comfortable silence. Once the water is warm enough for her, I pull her into the shower, and clean her up, taking my time.

She melts in my arms, letting me take care of her. I can't resist placing kisses all over her as I wash her up and rinse her off. Keeping my hands and mouth off her is going to be a never-ending struggle. She doesn't seem to mind.

She's pliant in my arms, purring like a little kitten while I wash her hair. I try to be gentle with the tangles so I don't hurt her. Gentleness seems to come a little easier the longer I'm around her, like being with her is breathing life back into that part of me that I thought I'd lost to the stench of war long ago. It wasn't lost though, simply buried. But the need to care for her overrides everything else, bringing that softer part of me to the surface.

The hot water doesn't last long. By the time I wash her up, it's lukewarm. But I've bathed in frigid lakes and worse. Spots of her blood stain my cock. The sight of it sends a wave of possessiveness through me. She's mine now, tied to me in ways that can never be undone.

I reluctantly wash off her blood before turning the water off and leading her out of the shower.

Once she's dry, I scoop her up in my arms and carry her to bed.

Her bedroom, like the rest of her house, is warm and inviting. Her four-poster bed dominates the small space. Her walls are a soft lavender and gray, with a brighter purple pentaptych hanging on the wall above the bed. Each of the five panels show part of the same watercolor scene. Her bedding matches the painting. The hardwood floor is covered in a plush rug that matches the gray in the walls. There's a small chair in one corner, and a dresser in the other, with matching tables on each side of the bed. The room is comforting more than girly, an oasis of tranquility.

I pull the covers back and lay her on the sheets, pressing a kiss to her temple. She curls up with a soft sigh, already on the verge of sleep. She looks so goddamn beautiful with her hair still damp, no makeup on her face, and my marks all over her. My dick stirs at the arresting sight, gearing up for another round. He's not going to be satisfied tonight. I already know she's going to be sore.

The reminder keeps me from crawling into the bed beside her. I backtrack out of the room into her bathroom. I prowl through her cabinets until I find a bottle of Tylenol and shake two out into my hand for her. I fill the little cup by the sink with water.

My shoulders are a mess of angry claw marks. I'm sure my back probably matches. She's a little lioness in bed, more than capable of taking me. I fucking love it.

She watches me with wide eyes as I stalk toward her, breathless all over again at how beautiful she is. Her body is incredible, lush in all the right ways. Her tits are more than a handful, her waist trim before flaring out to her wide hips. She was made to carry babies.

I hope I bred her the first time, hope my seed is already taking root.

"Sore?"

She shakes her head, her eyes drifting from mine.

"Liar," I mutter, holding the Tylenol out to her. "I was rough with you."

She licks her lips, meeting my gaze again. "You didn't hurt me. I liked it."

Thank God for that.

"Take these anyway," I order her, worried she'll wake up sore tomorrow if she doesn't. The thought of her in pain makes me feel like someone has a hook in my guts, twisting it.

She shakes her head at me but takes the Tylenol anyway. She hands the glass back to me when she's done.

"What's your code?"

"Hmm?"

"Alarm code. What is it?"

"Oh. 8675."

I stride out of the bedroom to lock up and arm the system. I'm more than capable of killing to protect her but having an alarm to alert me if anyone tries to get close will help me rest easy. Because I already know I'm not going to be able to do that with her here to protect. She's necessary for my survival now, far more precious than anything else in this world. I'll guard her with my dying breath.

I set the alarm, lock the door, and then gather up our clothes.

She's still awake, watching me with the same wide-eyed expression on her face when I make it back to the bedroom. I can see her mind working, see her trying to process my confession and the fact that she gave me her virginity. I don't rush her. That's not why I told her how I feel. I needed her to know that she matters to me, that my heart belongs to her.

I've been at war so long, I forgot what peace felt like. I gave up thinking the American Dream was something I could have too. I know better now. This brilliant, beautiful woman gives me what I haven't even let myself dream about before now: Peace. Hope. More. My future is in her hands, and I've got all the time in the world for her to realize she loves me.

I already know she does. She never would have spread those legs for me if she didn't. But she has to work it out for herself. She's been neglected by the world for far too long. She's skittish, afraid to trust. I'll wait however long I have to wait for her to let those walls come tumbling down completely.

I toss our clothes in the chair in the corner. She watches every move I make with those wide, sleepy eyes. She opens her mouth and then closes it. Does it again. She wants to say something. I wait her out, not rushing her.

I crawl into bed beside her before pulling her into my arms. She comes willingly, snuggling up against my chest. One arm slides across my abdomen, her feet tangling with mine beneath the covers. A sweet little sigh washes across my chest.

I reach over and turn off the lamp, casting the room into darkness.

Finally, she speaks.

"Did you mean what you said?"

"Yeah," I murmur, smiling in the dark. "I meant it."

She processes that for a minute, turning it over in her mind, absorbing it.

"Okay," she whispers then. "I..."

"Don't have to say anything," I say, cutting her off. "Didn't say it so you'd say it back. Just thought you should know where I stand. We've got time, as much as you need."

"Okay," she whispers again.

I kiss her on the forehead, and she settles back down in my arms, letting me hold her again. My hand drifts through her damp hair, my eyes drifting close.

This is heaven.

❧❧❧ ❧❧❧

"Is Liberty here yet?" I ask Kathy, stopping at her desk on my way in. I had to run home and change, so Liberty drove herself. I didn't like it. Holding her all night and waking up with her still in my arms was utter goddamn perfection. She looked so sweet this morning. I desperately wanted to fuck her, but I resisted the urge. She didn't like that much, but I know she needs a break.

Leaving her to go home was hell. Her place is small, but it's a home. Mine is just the place I go to at the end of the day. My shit is still in boxes, my walls bare. Maybe that's not a bad thing though. It means she'll be able to change whatever she wants, however she wants because her place isn't big enough for a family...and we're definitely going to have one of those.

The more I think about a future with her, the more I want it all.

"Haven't seen her," Kathy says, handing me a stack of checks. "Those need to be signed so I can get them in the mail. And the plumber called. He's trying to track down a part he needs to finish up in the kitchen. Also, the washer delivery will be here in twenty minutes."

I tuck the bag of food I picked up for Liberty under my arm to take the checks from Kathy. "Good. Call Stavros and tell him to meet me in A Wing in fifteen."

"Yes, sir."

I stride toward my office, eager to set eyes on Liberty before I tackle all the shit on my list for the day. She needs to move in with me sooner rather than later. This driving in different cars bullshit isn't going to work for me. I want her with me, where I can keep an eye on her.

I frown when I get to the office and see the lights are off. She's not here yet. I head inside, dropping the checks on my desk and her breakfast on hers. I doubt she had a chance to eat after I left. We were running late. Mostly because letting her put clothes on should be criminal. She's a goddess.

I drag my phone out of my pocket to call her.

"Hey," she answers on the third ring, breathless. "I'm running late. Traffic."

"You're moving in with me."

"What?"

"You're moving in with me," I repeat, adjusting the flowers on her desk so they're closer to the window. They probably need sunlight.

"You can't order me to move in with you, Killian," she says, her voice quiet.

"I'm not."

"It certainly sounds like it."

"I want you with me," I mutter, trying to ignore the twinge of hurt over the fact that she doesn't want to move in with me. I can't rush her. She needs time, and I know that. But I've never slept as peacefully as I did with her in my arms last night. Now that I've had it, I don't want to give it up. Don't want to go backwards when every fiber of my being demands we move forward. Moving in. Marriage. Babies.

"We barely know each other."

My brows snap together. "I know you well enough to know how you sound when you're coming all over me."

"That's not what I meant."

"No?"

She sighs into the phone. "You can't just bulldoze your way into my life, Killian. You can't make decisions for me and just expect me to fall in line. I'm not one of your soldiers."

Jesus. Is that what she thinks I'm doing? Bulldozing my way into her life? Trying to force her into more than she's ready to give me?

Have I been doing that?

I think back over the last two days, all the demands I've made. Telling her what's going to happen between us, telling her to stop overthinking it. Deciding when she eats and when she works and where she works.

Fuck.

Maybe I have been too demanding, trying to force her where I want her even while trying to convince myself that I'm giving her time. Making decisions is what I do. I don't spend a lot of time thinking things through or talking it out. I do what needs to be done. It's what I've always done, but this is different.

She's different. She's used to taking care of herself, of being the only one who decides her future. I can't just expect that to change overnight because I'm in love with her. If I want her to realize she loves me too, I have to back off and give her space.

"You're right," I mutter, blowing out a breath. "The choice should be yours."

"Killian—"

"I'll back off."

"Killian, that's not wha—"

"When you're ready, we'll talk about it. But not until." I glance at my watch, realize that I'm already running behind. "I need to go check on some shit. Your breakfast is on your desk when you get here. Drive safe."

"Okay," she whispers. There's something in her tone, but she disconnects before I have a chance to figure out what it is or what it means.

I tip my head back and curse. I hate knowing that she feels like I'm bulldozing my way into her life. I want to give her everything she's ever wanted, make her happy. Clearly, I'm not off to a great start. I need to regroup and make a new plan. Because now that I've had her, there's no way I can let her go.

I survived an IED blast and warzones. Epidemics and terrorists. I've been to hell and walked out alive. But there's no fucking way I'll survive without her. I'm so in love with her it's almost painful. Letting her go now isn't an option. So I need to figure out how to make her happy. Because her being unhappy isn't feeling much like an option either.

In fact, it's feeling pretty goddamn intolerable from where I'm standing.

Chapter Seven

LIBERTY

"I THINK I MESSED up."

"By taking the job? You can always tell him to suck an egg and come back here. I miss you. Dominic won't let me do anything fun," Summer says.

"Not by taking the job." I drop my head back against my desk chair and stare up at the ceiling. The spackling directly overhead looks like a duck. It's almost noon, but I haven't seen Killian. He's been running all over the place, putting out proverbial fires. He's texted me a few times. I think he's mad at me though. "I like Killian."

"And he turned out to be a jerk?" Summer asks, a little thread of iron in her voice. "I can send Dominic to kick his ass. What did he do? Maybe I'll kick his ass myself."

"He didn't do anything." I huff out a breath. "He's done everything right."

"Oh." Summer pauses. "So...what's the problem?"

"I slept with him."

"What? Seriously? Holy crap."

"Yeah," I whisper. "I'm in love with him."

"Well, obviously," she says with a little laugh. "You wouldn't have slept with him if you weren't. Was it good? What am I saying? Of course it was. I refuse to believe a man like him is bad at sex."

"He's definitely not bad at it," I mutter, my cheeks heating. If anything, he might be too good at it because I want to do it over and over with him. The way I felt with him inside me was indescribable. I've never felt as close to anyone as I did with him last night. Even afterward, when he took care of me, I felt cherished, adored. I never want that feeling to end. But I think I messed it up this morning. "He told me he loved me."

"Aww, of course he does! You're incredible and you're gorgeous. He would be an idiot if he didn't love you. Everyone does."

I snort.

"I'm serious, Liberty," she says. "You don't see it because being alone is all you know, but everyone loves you. Dominic didn't hire you just because you're smart. He hired you because he knew you needed a safe place to land and a family. There isn't a single person here who wouldn't miss you if you left."

"I didn't know that," I admit.

"I know," Summer says. "You're not very good at letting yourself be loved."

She's right. I've always been too afraid to get too close, scared I'd get attached and then be left alone again. It's the life I know. I moved from foster home to foster home, never staying for long. I got attached to some of the families at first, but they never kept me. Eventually, I stopped trying to become part of the family, to get close. It was easier that way.

When I finally got accepted to the boarding school, it was a relief because I had a sense of permanence. I kept to myself though. Just in case my caseworker decided to pull me out and move me. I worked hard to maintain good grades so she wouldn't have a reason to move me.

Until Summer started working for Dom, I did the same thing there...threw myself into the work. I tell myself that's because I didn't want to get fired, but I think Summer is right. I did it because I'm not good at letting myself be loved, at letting people in.

I hide because it's easier. But I don't want to do that this time. I'm so in love with Killian. I knew it before he ever told me he felt the same. But I didn't say it back. I was too scared to do it, to let myself be that vulnerable with him.

"He wants me to move in with him."

"Wow."

"I want to do it," I whisper, swallowing. "But I didn't tell him that. I panicked." I feel so bad about what I said to him. I know I hurt his feelings, even if he never admits it. I wanted to say yes, tell him that I love him too. Instead, I freaked out, accused him of bulldozing his way into my life.

I *love* that he takes charge and doesn't let me hide from him. I love that he's constantly in my space and how confidently he makes decisions. I didn't say any of that though. I should have. Because now he thinks I want space, and that's the exact opposite of what I want.

"You're afraid," Summer guesses, her voice soft.

"So afraid," I admit, tears burning at the backs of my eyes. "I've never met anyone like him before. I don't want to move too fast and ruin this. But I don't want to move slow either. I don't want him to regret falling for me."

"Liberty," Summer whispers.

"It sounds stupid out loud."

"It doesn't. Do you remember when I was going to quit?"

"Yes." How can I forget it? She was miserable, thinking Dom didn't love her.

"I was afraid to tell Dominic how I felt, afraid that I'd ruin things if I did. I decided that I'd rather leave than have him find out that I was crazy about him. I was wrong then," she admits. "I think you're wrong now. You're so worried that he'll regret falling for you that you're pushing him away. You're making your own regrets, trying to save him from those you think he might have."

"I'm..." I swallow the instinctive denial because she's right. That *is* what I'm doing. I told him that he can't make decisions for me, but I'm trying to do the same thing for him. Worse, I'm treating him like he doesn't know his own mind, when he's made it clear over and over that he does. That he wants me. That he loves me. I'm putting my insecurities on his shoulders, when it's my hang-ups that are the problem.

And he's been so patient, so understanding. He knows I'm scared, and he doesn't get mad at me for it. He just reminds me that he's here and that everything will be fine.

God, I'm so blind.

He's been nothing short of incredible to me, and I pushed him away.

Which means it's on me to fix it.

"I need to go," I tell Summer, already formulating a plan. "Call you later?"

"Of course. Love you."

"Love you too."

"Whoa," she says. "You've never said it back before. You always just say you too."

"I'm trying something new."

"I like it."

I smile. "Thank you, Summer. For everything. You're my best friend and I appreciate you so much. I don't know if I've ever told you that before, but it's true."

"You're going to make me cry!"

"No crying. I have a Marine to catch."

"Have fun."

I disconnect and sit there for a moment, thinking. He's been avoiding me, giving me space. It's my turn to take the lead and let him know how I feel for once. It's my turn to take a leap and put my heart on the line like he's done for me. And I know exactly what to do to show him how much I want to be with him.

I glance at the clock. It's almost noon. If I hurry, I can get what I need and get back before the hour is up. I grab my purse and slip my feet back into my shoes before grabbing my phone and heading out.

Kathy's at the front desk when I get there. She looks up at me, the phone stuck to her ear.

"Lunch," I mouth to her.

She gives me a thumbs up.

I duck out the front door into the sunshine, checking to make sure Killian isn't close. The parking lot is empty. He's probably still dealing with the plumber or one of the other thousand things that require his attention. He's putting in so much hard work to make this program a success. It's honestly impressive how much he's managed to accomplish in so short a time.

The people who find a place here are fortunate to have him in their corner. God knows, I'm lucky to have him in mine. No one has ever treated me like he does or made me as happy as he does. He may be rough around the edges, but that gruff personality of his hides a heart of gold. One that he's entrusted to me.

I hurry to my car as quickly as I can. My legs are a little stiff from sitting for so long and my thighs and pussy are a little sore from last night. I don't regret it though. I love that I'm carrying a little reminder of him today, especially since he refused to budge on doing it again this morning. I tried to convince him, but he's very stubborn.

I love that about him.

Hell, who am I kidding?

I love everything about him.

By the time I get to the house to get what I need and head back toward work, my lunch break is almost over. I thought it would take far less time to get there and get back, but traffic is crazy. Everyone seems to be on the road, rushing to get food.

I swing by Panera to grab us some lunch. Killian is probably starving by now. I know I am. I tried to eat the breakfast he bought me, but I didn't have much of an appetite after what I said to him on the phone.

My stomach growls when I'm back in the car with the food. The soup smells amazing.

My phone rings when I'm a couple blocks from the office.

I fish it out of my purse and smile when I see Killian's name on the screen.

"Hey," I murmur, hitting the Bluetooth button so it syncs to the stereo and I don't have to try to juggle the phone and drive.

"You left without me," he growls.

"You were busy." I frown, not sure why he's so worked up about it. I haven't been gone very long and I'm already almost back to the facility. It's literally a block away.

I flip my blinker on to get in the left lane so I can turn.

"I wanted to have lunch with you."

"Oh." My heart melts a little when I hear the pout in his voice...which he will never admit is there. It's sweet though. "I didn't eat. I picked us up lunch. I figured you were probably hungry."

"I'm starving, baby girl. And I don't want food."

"Oh." I press my thighs together to ease the ache his growl sends tearing through me. Thank God I'm at a red light because I can't see through the haze of desire.

"You still mad at me?"

"I wasn't ever mad at you, Killian. Um, can we talk when I get back to the office?"

"Why?"

"Because I have some things to say."

"Depends on if you can talk while I'm fucking you with my tongue."

"Killian!"

"Been thinking about it all day, baby girl. Can't concentrate on a fucking thing because I keep remembering how good you taste and how sweet you sound." His breath rasps down the line. "I fucking hate giving you space."

"It's not my favorite thing either," I admit, easing off the brake when the car in front of me turns. I follow behind it, eager to get back to the office to see him. "I've missed you so damn much today, Killian."

"Yeah?"

"Yeah. I haven't gotten anything done because I can't concentrate. Can we start o...Oh my gosh!" I shout, shocked when a black SUV barrels through the light, headed right at me. I hit the gas, trying to get out of the way, but it's already too late. He's going too fast and I'm barely moving.

The SUV plows into me, the screech of metal ripping through the air.

I scream Killian's name.

Chapter Eight

KILLIAN

"L iberty!" I yell, listening in horror as she screams for me. The sound of metal scraping on metal is loud...too loud. I've been pacing around the parking lot like a caged beast, waiting for her to get back. She's close though. The sound of the impact is too loud to be coming just from the phone.

I take off running toward the roadway, frantic to get to her. God, if she's hurt. If I lose her...

My breath rasps in my throat, erupting in an enraged roar at the thought. I can't lose her. She's everything that's right in my world. I knew it the moment I saw her. Spending the morning away from her only reinforced how important she is to me. I've been on edge all day, fucking hating the way we left shit between us this morning.

I reach the roadway and whip my head back and forth. I see the SUV sitting in the middle of the intersection, the front end dented. I don't see Liberty or her car though. God, where is she?

"Jesus. Oh, Jesus," I rasp, running full out in that direction.

Cars are pulled over on the side of the roadway. I dodge them, moving as quickly as I can to get to her. By the time I make it to the intersection, my lungs burn and my heart pounds a frenetic rhythm against my ribcage. My stomach is twisted in knots, terror for her churning through me with every beat of my heart.

I round the side of the SUV and see her car sitting sideways, facing the wrong direction. The back end is all fucked up. The back axel is destroyed, the back tire sitting at an odd angle. There's probably frame damage.

It doesn't matter. She's the only thing that matters right now. The driver's side door is standing open and she isn't inside.

"Liberty!" I shout, whipping my head back and forth, trying to find her in the milling crowd. I'm ready to lose my damn mind when I see her through a break in the crowd. She's sitting on the sidewalk, surrounded by people.

I shout her name again and race toward her, shoving people out of the way. She doesn't look hurt, but she's pale. Too pale. She's got her arms wrapped around her middle. She looks so damn tiny and fragile.

"Liberty," I rasp.

She looks up at me.

"Killian," she cries when she sees me. Tears fill her eyes and then spill over.

I drop to my knees in front of her, dragging her into my arms. She burrows into me, sobbing and clinging to me like she's afraid I'll disappear if she lets me go. As soon as she's in my arms, the vise around my heart loosens.

She's safe.

"Are you hurt, baby girl?" I ask, running my hands all over her to make sure.

"N-no. Just scared."

"Shh. I've got you," I promise, glaring at everyone until they look away, giving us a modicum of privacy. I bury my face in her hair, breathe in that sweet coconut scent...send up a prayer of gratitude to God for keeping her safe for me.

Sirens finally sound in the distance, letting me know the cops are on the way. Which is probably a good thing. If I get my hands on whoever hit her, I'm killing them. The other driver is lucky she isn't hurt. It's the only thing keeping me calm right now.

Liberty hears the sirens and sniffles before pulling back. Her eyes are rimmed in red, little streaks of mascara down her cheeks. I wipe it off with shaking hands, putting her back together so she can meet the world on her feet, as the courageous woman she is. She doesn't like to cry or let anyone see her vulnerability. And that's okay. I'll help protect that fragile part of her with my life, let her be the brilliant woman she is when other people are around.

"What happened?" I ask her, pressing my lips to her forehead and then both of her cheeks and her lips. Letting her go isn't an option right now. Or ever. If she isn't ready to move in with me, I'll move in with her. Or sleep on her porch. Whatever it takes to make her realize that this is permanent and I'm not going anywhere without her.

"He r-ran the red light," she says, hiccupping. "I tried to get out of the way, but there was a car in front of me so I couldn't move fast enough." Her honey-colored eyes meet mine. "I was so scared I'd never get to see you again."

"That'll never happen," I promise, touching my mouth to hers. "You're mine now, baby girl. Nothing is allowed to take you from me. I won't allow it."

She stares at me for a moment, and then her lips quirk up into a tremulous smile. "I almost believe you could do it, that you could keep everything from touching me. Killian, I..."

And I know what she's going to say. I see it blazing in her eyes.

"Not here," I rasp, placing my fingers against her lips.

She studies me for a moment and then nods her understanding.

* * *

After the police officer gets her statement, I send her back to the office to wait for me while I deal with her car. It's more than likely going to be a complete loss. The other driver, a father of four, is fortunate that she reacted as quick as she did to get out of the way, or it would have been a lot worse. He was doing well over the speed limit, trying to get to school to pick up a sick kid.

The fact that he was rushing to get his kid is the only thing that saved him from my wrath. That and the fact that Liberty is okay. She's shaken up, but otherwise unharmed. She may be a little sore tomorrow, but I had the paramedics check her out and they said she's going to be just fine.

I might not be though. It's going to be decades before I'm ready to let her out of my sight. And I already know that isn't going to work for her. Which means I'm going to be a miserable son of a bitch every time she leaves the house. I'll find a way to deal with it though. Whatever it takes.

By the time I've got the car towed, it's close to three. I catch a ride back to the office with the wrecker and then head inside.

"She's in the office," Kathy says, not even waiting for me to ask.

"Thanks." I jerk my chin in a nod and head that way, ready to get my girl and get her home for the day. No point in staying for the rest of the day when I already know I'm not going to get a fucking thing done. I just want to get her home and get in her bed. Everything else can wait until tomorrow.

I stop in the doorway and stare at her. Anyone else would be too shaken up to get anything done, but not Liberty. She's behind her desk, hard at work on her magic code. Her bottom lip is caught between her teeth, her eyes narrowed as she types away.

My gaze drifts from her to the old duffle bag beside her desk. I'm not sure what's in it, but she was adamant that she needed it. I figure she'll tell me about it when she's ready, but I'm curious.

"Dammit," she mutters under her breath, glaring at her screen. "Stupid not-magic code."

I chuckle, drawing her eyes. They light up when they land on me, which makes my dick rock hard in about two seconds flat. Jesus. I hope she never stops looking at me like that.

"You're back," she says.

"I am." I push away from the door and prowl toward her. "Do you want to finish what you're working on, or do you want to go home, baby girl?"

A frown crosses her face, crinkling her brows. "What do you want to do?"

"Whatever you want."

She huffs at me, clearly not liking that response. "Tell me."

"I want to take you home, put you in bed, and keep you there until I forget the way you screamed my name," I admit, stopping beside her desk.

She swallows hard, leaning her head back to look at me. "I screamed for you because I knew you would find me and make everything better," she whispers. "You were the only thing I wanted when he hit me."

"Jesus." I clench my hands into fists, trying to keep myself from ripping her out of the chair and fucking her against the wall. Can't do that though. She needs soft and gentle right now.

"I also screamed for you because I thought I'd never..." She pauses for a second and then reaches out for me.

I take her invitation, picking her up out of her chair to take her place. I pull her down with me, cuddling her up against my chest. It takes a little maneuvering before we're both comfortable, but I could sit on a bed of lava and feel no pain so long as she was in my lap.

She sighs her contentment and rests her head against my shoulder for a moment before she pulls back to meet my gaze. "I screamed your name because I thought I'd never get to tell you that I love you," she says, her eyes shining with moisture. "I thought I was going to die without you knowing how I feel about you. I love you, Killian. So much."

"I know you do, baby girl," I murmur, my voice husky with emotion. Jesus. I've gone from hell to heaven in the space of a single afternoon. "Just been waiting for you to realize it too."

"I knew." She bites her lip. "I don't know how to let people love me or let myself be loved, but I want to change that. I didn't mean what I said this morning."

"You were right."

"No, I wasn't." She shakes her head. "I panicked and said something I didn't mean. I *love* the way you are with me. You know what I need, and you just give it to me. I know that you'll take care of me because you always do. Even when I wouldn't put myself first, you put me first. I've never had that before," she whispers, tears pooling in her eyes. "I love it so much, and I was afraid if we moved too fast, you might regret being with me. Everyone leaves, and I don't want you to leave me too."

"Never," I growl, wiping her tears away with my thumbs.

"I forgot one important thing though, Killian."

"What thing?"

She wiggles around until we're sharing the same sliver of air. Her forehead touches mine, her eyes fluttering like they want to close. She keeps them open though, watching me intently.

"What thing?" I ask again, locking my hands into place on the arms of the chair to keep myself from stripping her naked. She's wrecking me and she doesn't even have a clue. I think I've been waiting for her my entire life, waiting to find her and love her. Now that she's mine, I'm constantly torn between fucking her raw and taking care of her. Every word from her lips sends the scale tipping wildly, first in one direction and then the other.

"That *I'll* regret it if I don't move in with you."

My entire body goes stock still. I even stop breathing for a second as her confession works its way through me, blowing like a hot breeze through my veins. I lean back so I can see her face and read her expression. Certainty shines in her honey-eyes. There's no doubt there, no fear. She means it.

I really am in heaven.

"Going to kiss you now," I mutter.

"Wait!" She throws her hand up, placing it on my chest.

It halts me in my tracks.

"I need to show you something first," she says and then points at her bag. "Can you hand me that, please?"

I hesitate for a moment, really wanting to kiss the shit out of her, but then curiosity wins out. I reach down and snag the bag off of the floor. There's nowhere to put it, so I set it on the desk. She wiggles around until I reluctantly stand her up.

"You should open this," she says, holding the bag out to me.

I cock my head to the side, growing more curious by the minute. She doesn't say anything though, just waits for me to take it from her. I set it in my lap and tug the zipper down. I'm not sure what I expected, but clothes wasn't at the top of the list.

"Clothes?"

"Not those," she says, pulling them out and setting them to the side. "Well, those are important too, but it's the other stuff in there I want you to see."

I glance from her back to the bag. I pull out an old photo album, a stuffed rabbit that's so old the fur has started to turn yellow, and then a small shadow box with a Purple Heart in it. Underneath the medal is a small plaque.

"Oliver D. Connor," I read, glancing up at her.

"My dad." She reaches out to touch the edge of the box. "It's his medal."

"Didn't know he was a recipient," I murmur.

"Yeah. He received it after his men were ambushed on a mission. He was shot, but he carried one of his men to safety, refusing to leave him behind. He was stubborn like that." A ghost of a smile twists at her lips. "When I realized that they were taking me away from him, I stole it from his room to take with me. It meant so much to him. I thought if I took it, it meant he would find me."

"Jesus," I whisper.

"I've had it packed in that bag since the day I went into foster care. Everything in there, I've kept in there all this time. I wanted to be ready to go if he ever came for me." She swallows hard, staring at the shadow box. "Even after they told me he'd died, I kept it packed."

"Why?"

She swallows again. "At first, I did it because I didn't believe he was really gone. And then I left it packed so it would always be ready when it was time for me to move to the next home. I told myself that I'd unpack it when I found the place I was meant to be, but I never found that place." She swipes at her eyes, brushing away the tears trembling in her lashes. "I've lived in my house for over a year, but I still haven't unpacked it."

She's killing me. Breaking my heart one little piece at a time. I hate that she grew up that way, never feeling like she had a home or a place where she belonged.

"I want to unpack it now, Killian," she whispers. "Because I've finally found where I belong."

"Where, baby girl?" I rasp, reaching for her to draw her closer.

"With you." She smiles at me. "I belong with you. Wherever you go, that's where I belong. That's my home because you're there."

Fuck.

I swallow convulsively and quickly place everything back in the old bag, moving quickly. Once it's all packed away again, including the clothes she has clutched to her chest, I set it carefully aside and then pull her down onto my lap.

My lips meet hers as I pour my soul into that kiss, into her. It's all hers anyway. I set out to possess her, to make her my own. Instead, she made me hers. My heart beats for her now, beats because of her. If I'm her home, she's my heaven, my own little piece of paradise.

And I'm never giving it up.

Chapter Nine

LIBERTY

"WHAT DO YOU THINK?" I ask Killian, stepping back to run a critical eye over my handiwork. It's not half bad. At least I don't think so. I'm not sure what he thinks.

He steps up behind me, wrapping his arms around my waist. I melt into his embrace, letting him hold me as he examines the room, quietly taking it all in.

"Looks good," he finally grunts, which makes me smile.

I glance around the bedroom again, relieved that he likes all the changes. When he brought me home two weeks ago, I realized that I'm not the only one who's been packed up and ready to move on. All of his stuff was still in boxes, sitting untouched.

We've spent the last two weeks changing that. When we aren't at work, we're here, fixing this place up. I just put the finishing touches on the master suite, turning it into our own little paradise. My painting hangs on the wall over my bed because he said it's more comfortable than his. We moved his bedroom furniture to the guest bedroom but kept the couch he had in here.

Our stuff is all mixed together now, making this place our home. And I love it so much. The house is a beautiful Spanish Colonial situated near the northwestern shore of Lake Murray. The big iron fence surrounding the property makes it feel a little like we're in a world of our own out here. It's quiet and peaceful without being too isolated. It's the best of both worlds.

"I need to see one thing," he mutters, tilting my head to place a kiss on the side of my throat. He steers me toward the bed, licking and biting me.

"Killian," I moan, already knowing what he's after. He's said the same thing about virtually every room in the house right before stripping me naked to make love to me. He hasn't found a room he doesn't like seeing me naked in.

"You know the rule," he growls, swatting me on the ass. "Clothes off and legs spread, baby girl."

I moan, heat unfurling inside me. He helps strip me down, running his rough hands all over my body as he goes. By the time I'm naked, I'm already soaked and trembling with desire. Somehow, he always leaves me this way. I don't think I'll ever grow tired of how badly I want him or how much I love when he's inside me.

He was gentle right after the accident, afraid he'd hurt me. He's not afraid now.

He picks me up and drops me on the bed, staring at my pussy while he undresses. I watch him just as intently, staring shamelessly as he reveals his body to me. He's built like a warrior, all those muscles ready for war.

He wraps his fist around his cock, jerking himself off with rough pulls.

I moan his name, reaching out for him.

"You want my cock?" he asks, prowling toward me.

"Yes. Please, Killian. Please. I need it."

He likes it when I beg him. It drives him crazy, makes his control slip a little. I love that I do that to him. That I can unravel him with a few simple words. Precum wells from the slit of his cock. He curses, stalking toward me.

I expect him to crawl up on the bed with me, but he doesn't. He grabs my ankles and pulls me toward him, until my ass is hanging off the side of the bed and I'm clutching at the covers to keep myself from tumbling into the floor.

I don't have to worry about it though. I already know he isn't going to let me fall.

He kneels beside the bed, running his lips up the inside of my leg. His stubble scratches at my skin, making my flesh pebble. I moan his name, reaching out to touch him.

He smacks my pussy.

"Killian!" I jolt upward as pleasure shoots through me.

"You know you aren't allowed to touch me yet," he growls. "Not until I eat you."

He never lets me get my hands on him too soon, no matter how hard I try. And I do try. I fight him every step of the way sometimes, both because I really want to touch him and because he loves it when I fight him. Nothing makes him harder than when I fight to get my hands on him. I love it too. He fucks me so hard when he finally gets inside me.

Most of the time, I give him what he wants because taking care of me makes him happy. But when we're alone, I make him work for it. That naughty side he woke up inside me that first day has only grown in the last couple of weeks. He's teaching me so much about myself, waking parts of me I didn't even know existed, desires I've never had before.

He's dirty and rough and so damn incredible.

He smacks my pussy again, making me moan his name.

"Dirty little girl," he growls before yanking me onto his mouth. He doesn't take it slow, but dives right in, eating me like he hasn't had a taste of me in weeks instead of a mere few hours. He grunts and growls against my center, using his lips and teeth and tongue to turn me into a frenzy of need. He spreads my cheeks, burying his face between them.

I cry out his name, writhing as he eats me there too. I'm not sure which of us loves it more. It feels so damn good.

Everything he does to me feels like heaven. My body is littered with his marks. Mine are scored into his skin.

He thrusts his tongue into my pussy, fucking me with it until I'm right on the edge.

"Killian," I groan in protest when he backs off right before I slip over the edge.

He slides me back onto the bed and then flips me over onto my stomach. His hand comes down hard against my ass. I tilt it higher, rocking back for more. My nipples drag across the bedspread, making me moan.

"Up on your hands and knees, Liberty," he growls, yanking my ass up higher.

I scramble to obey, desperate to feel him inside me again. Not that he ever really leaves. When he slips from my body, he always leaves a little bit of himself behind. I spend my days coated in his come. My Marine is filthy, but I love every minute of it.

He wraps an arm around my waist, pulling me closer to the edge of the bed. Once he has me where he wants me, I feel him spreading my cheeks apart again.

"Goddamn," he growls. "These little pink holes look good in this room, Liberty. You gonna keep them on display for me?"

"Y-yes."

"Good." He reaches around me to grab a pillow, slipping it underneath me. "Lay on this and spread your cheeks for me. I want to look at what's mine while I'm nine deep."

Oh my goodness.

My cheeks heat at the thought of him staring at me down there, but I leap to obey anyway. Whatever gets him inside me faster.

I'm barely in place, my cheek to the pillow while I spread my cheeks open for him with my hands, when his cock nudges at my entrance. He taps it against my clit, slicking it up with the juices I feel wetting my thighs. And then he's thrusting deep.

I cry out his name, rocking forward with the force of his thrust. My hands almost slip, but I manage to keep them where they are, holding myself open for his licentious gaze. I don't even have to see his face to know he's staring at me there. I can feel the heat of his gaze.

"Fuck," he grunts, pounding into me hard and fast. His hips crash into my ass, digging my fingers into my flesh. Every thrust has my nipples dragging across the bed, and the pillow sliding from beneath my face.

I moan his name, already climbing toward the peak. He gets me there so easily. In two weeks, he's learned more about my body and what I like than I ever knew. He knows how to get me off in a matter of minutes. That's okay though because I never go alone. When I come, he always goes over with me. He loves and hates it in turns.

"Tell me," he orders me.

"I love you."

"Again."

"I love you!"

"Fuck. Yeah, you do." He spits on my asshole, slicking it up. And then his hand is there, his thumb pressing against the tight ring of muscle...pressing into me. He fingers my ass while he fucks me.

I writhe beneath him, calling out his name as my body overheats and my inner walls clench around him, trying to pull him in even deeper.

"Going to claim you here as soon as I get you pregnant," he tells me, replacing his thumb with his fingers. "Make sure this hole knows who it belongs to like the rest of them do."

"Killian, oh my God."

He shoves his free hand underneath me to play with my clit. "Going to tie you up when I take you here. Only way I can keep you still. You go wild as soon as I get in you, baby girl." He presses his thumb to my clit at the same time he thrusts his fingers into me. "Fuck. You're going to come on me, aren't you?"

"Y-y-yes!" I sob, wracked by pleasure. He's everywhere, claiming every part of me all at once. It's intense, sending me racing toward a massive orgasm. It's almost terrifying how big it is...but I want it anyway.

"Do it, baby girl," he growls, fucking me hard enough to rattle the bed frame. "Give me what belongs to me."

He presses his thumb to my clit again, twisting his fingers inside me.

I scream his name as pleasure rips me wide open. I thrash and wail my way through it, screaming myself raw as it roars through me, stealing the breath from my lungs. I hear him roaring my name, hear myself sobbing his back at him, but I'm frozen in place, caught in a fierce net of pleasure that goes on and on forever, detonating inside me again and again.

He pumps his hips, filling me full of him. It splashes out, making a mess of both of us. Still, he keeps pumping his hips, moaning my name. I writhe through it, riding out the waves as his cock jerks inside me over and over.

When the last drop splashes inside me, I fall limp beneath him, sucking in air in heaving gulps. My lungs and throat burn, but the rest of me feels fuzzy and far away, muted. He groans my name again and then slumps over me, resting his sweaty head against my back.

"Liberty," he whispers. "God, baby girl."

We stay just like that for several moments, trying to catch our breath. Once he does, he reluctantly pulls out of me, running a soothing hand down my hip. I hear him moving across the floor but can't find the energy to open my eyes to see where he's going.

I float in that delicious void for several minutes, too blissed out to care about much of anything. I swear, he recovers a lot faster than I do. He has enough energy for the both of us most days. I get sleepy after I come, but he could go for hours.

A few minutes later, I hear him walking back toward me. He flips me over onto my back and then scoops me up in his strong arms. He holds me close to his chest, cradling me like I'm precious cargo. I close my eyes and drift, confident that wherever he's taking me will be good.

With him, I don't have to worry. He does it for me. I never really thought about how freeing that would feel, the lack of concern. But it is. For the first time in my life, there is no fear or anxiety, no stress. He helps me carry it.

I hear water running a split second before he's easing me down into the tub. The hot water closes over me, making me hum in contentment.

"Careful," he murmurs. He holds me steady before sliding into the massive tub with me and then pulling me back into his arms. His lips ghost across my forehead and then my cheeks. "You still awake, baby girl?"

"Mmhmm," I hum.

"Good. Open your eyes for me."

I grumble a protest, which makes him chuckle.

"Open them, Liberty."

I huff and then do what he wants. It takes a minute for me to peel them open. And then another for me to actually focus them. When I do, I blink. There are candles and rose petals everywhere, turning the bathroom into an oasis.

"Killian," I whisper.

"You like it?"

I nod, turning around on his lap until I can see his face. He's got it tilted down to me, my favorite smile on his lips.

"When did you do this?"

"Just now."

I blink at him, which makes that smile widen.

"You were out of it," he says, satisfaction glinting in his crystalline eyes. "Pretty sure you went to sleep on me." He cups my cheek, brushing strands of hair away from my face. "I got you something."

"You don't have to get me anything. This is perfect." It's more than that. God, the way this man loves me is incredible. Every day, I feel cherished. Every day, I fall deeper into love with him. It's been two weeks, but it feels like I've belonged to him for a lifetime.

"So you don't want this?" he says, reaching over to the side of the tub to grab something. He brings his hand up and turns it over, uncurling his fingers.

I gasp when I see the ring sitting on his palm. It's a solitary round diamond on a platinum band. It's gorgeous and so much bigger than any diamond I've ever seen outside of a movie. I lift my hand to touch it and then hesitate, not sure if I'm supposed to do that or not. I'm pretty sure he's asking me to marry him. Maybe I should wait until he says it first.

"Take it, baby girl," he says. "It's yours."

"Are you—?"

"Am I what?"

"Is this—?"

Amusement dances in his eyes and across his lips. He's laughing at me.

"You aren't very funny," I mutter, glaring at him.

He chuckles, reaching for my hand.

"You love me," he reminds me, slipping the ring onto my finger. It fits perfectly. "And you're marrying me."

I briefly consider teasing him since he's teasing me, but quickly decide against it.

"Okay," I say.

He cocks a brow, suspicious. "That was easy."

"I can say no if you want."

He growls at me.

"I want to marry you, Killian," I whisper, letting him off the hook. "I'm not saying no. I'm not even going to complain that you didn't even ask me. I'm just going to say yes. I love you. I love being with you. Yes, I'm marrying you."

"Fuck." He tips my head back, pressing a hard kiss to my lips.

I touch my tongue to his bottom lip, which makes him growl and deepen the kiss. My hands slide through his hair as I twist around on his lap until I'm straddling him. We kiss for a long, perfect moment before he pulls back to rest his forehead against mine.

"You're really going to marry me?"

"Yeah," I say, smiling. "I'm really going to marry you."

"Fuck," he whispers again, his eyes falling closed. "I love you, Liberty. Didn't think it was possible to be this goddamn happy, but with you, I am, baby girl. Every day, I'm happier than I ever have been before."

"I know," I whisper, running my hands through his hair again. "It's heaven, isn't it?"

"No."

"No?"

He shakes his head. "Being inside you is heaven. This is something else altogether. It's..."

"Home," I finish for him.

"Yeah," he agrees, his smile blinding. "This is home."

Epilogue

KILLIAN

ONE YEAR LATER

"Is that him?" Sebastian asks, grinning at me as the nurse slips inside Liberty's room with my son in her arms.

I take him from her, holding him carefully. They say he's big, but he's still tiny if you ask me. I could probably hold him in one hand, which I won't do because you have to hold babies carefully. They're fragile.

As soon as he's in my arms, pride swells in my chest. He's sleeping, his little lips pursed. He's as perfect as his mom. And she gets more perfect every single day. The last year of my life has been better than perfect. Every day, I love her more. She's the sun in my world...and our little boy is the moon. Both vital, both beautiful.

She's resting peacefully in the hospital bed beside me. She hasn't gotten much of that the last few weeks. She says it's impossible to get comfortable with a baby digging his toes into your ribs. I'm taking her word for it. But she never complained. Not once through her pregnancy did she complain.

She's the strongest person I know.

"He's so little," Kennedy whispers, reaching out to touch his hand.

"He looks like you," Caroline says, smiling.

"He's much cuter than Killian," Sebastian says, fucking with me. I see the look in his dark eyes though. See the way they move from me to his wife, lingering on her growing belly. He can't wait for his own baby to get here. She's not far behind. Their little girl is due any day now.

"What's his name?" Rowan asks, cuddling up against Sebastian's chest with her hand on her belly.

"Spencer."

"Aww," Kennedy and Caroline say at the same time.

"After her mom?" Rowan asks.

I nod. Nothing else fit right. Spencer is perfect though, a little piece of Liberty's mom that she can pass on to our children. She still doesn't talk much about her past, but it doesn't hurt her as much now as it used to. She talks about her parents sometimes, about the happy times they shared and how much they loved each other and loved her. I think she knows that her dad never stopped loving her. He just lost his way.

It helps her to see the men and women we serve, to hear their stories. She spends most of her time working out of my office now. Alessi doesn't seem to mind. He thinks it's good for her. Hell, I do too. She's blossomed in the last year, becoming a fierce advocate for veterans. They love her, which is a never-ending source of irritation for me. I love that my wife has people in her corner, but I'm still a jealous, possessive motherfucker. I think, if anything were to happen to me, she'd have a whole army at her back, ready to help take care of her for me.

That's the only reason I let the men in our care close to my wife. She deserves the peace that comes with knowing she isn't alone in this world. And she isn't alone in this world. With me at her side, she will never be alone again.

I've loved seeing her grow over the last year. She knows her worth now, knows how important she is and how much she is loved. That confidence never really leaves her eyes now. She's happy. Happier than I've ever seen her. And I love every minute of it.

"You did good, brother," Sebastian murmurs to me while the girls all coo over Spencer.

"I did, didn't I?" I say, smiling down at the baby in my arms. Hell, I did better than good. I hit the fucking lottery when I found Liberty. My wife is a goddess, and my son is perfect.

When I was in the desert and tried to envision a future for myself, I never could do it. I'm not sure if that's because

I didn't know Liberty was out there waiting for me to find her, or if it's because I couldn't even comprehend the kind of happiness I've found with her. But if I had been able to imagine it, it would have looked like this.

My son in my arms, my siblings around me, and my wife resting peacefully at my side.

This is what we fought for. This is what so many died for. This is the dream.

And it is so fucking beautiful.

Authors Note

IF YOU ENJOYED THE story, please consider leaving a review. They are such a huge help to authors!

Teaching Rowan, the second book in the Claimed series, is now available!

Teaching Rowan

Breaking the rules never felt so good.

Sebastian

Rowan Lassiter is pure magic.

I was under her spell the moment she opened her mouth.

But she's a teacher, and I'm her boss.

The rules say she's off-limits...that dating her is out of the question.

I guess it's a good thing a little scandal never hurt anyone, right?

Because no one is going to tell me I can't keep what belongs to me.

Rowan

All I've ever wanted to do is teach.

Right up until I ran straight into Dr. Sebastian Thorne, our new Superintendent.

Falling for him would be crazy, especially since the principal already hates me.

But I think it might already be too late for that.

Because all I want to do now is lose myself in him and the way he makes me feel.

Baby Jesus, please don't make me choose between him and the kids I love.

I promise I'll never ask for anything else.

Warning

When this curvy teacher runs right into her older billionaire boss, sparks fly. If instalove, rule-breaking, and over-the-top billionaires make you happy, get ready to take notes from Sebastian and Rowan in this hilariously sweet, steamy romance from Nichole Rose. As always, a sticky sweet and guaranteed HEA is coming your way.

Adore You

EXCERPT

I glance back toward the mechanical bull just in time to see a blonde go flying off onto the mats. She lays there for a long moment, laughing like she's having the time of her life. She's insane if you ask me.

No free shot and photo on the wall of achievement is worth all that.

"You thinkin' about riding, Minnie?"

I look over to the left and then blink at the man sitting in the far back corner of the booth next to ours. He's got his arm propped up on the back of the booth I'm in, a beer in his hands. I don't know how I missed him back there because there is nothing forgettable or missable about him. The left side of face is partially obscured in shadow, but his full lips and wide, angular jaw are visible. So is his close-cropped blond hair and deep-set, steel blue eyes.

He's big and brawny, like a cage fighter or a Viking. The sleeves of his button down are rolled up, showing off the tattoos crawling like ivy up his sun-kissed forearm. The way he wraps his long fingers around his bottle, gripping it firmly, makes me want to squirm, but I'm not sure why. He just seems so...commanding or controlled, maybe. Like nothing fazes him.

"I didn't see you there," I say.

"I know." He flashes me a smile, it's no more than a quick curving of one side of his mouth, but I feel like squirming again. He's beautiful in the same way wild animals are. Power and grace all wrapped up in a lethal, gorgeous package. "You didn't answer my question, Minnie."

"Miranda," I correct.

"Miranda." His lips curve again. "You got a last name, baby?"

Oh, jeez. I like that endearment coming out of his mouth way too much. It sounds delicious in his worn-leather tone.

"Dawson." The lie slips out without my permission

"Miranda Dawson. I'm Jason Kirby."

"It's nice to meet you, Jason Kirby." I smirk at him.

He watches me over the rim of his bottle as he brings it to his lips and takes a sip.

I squirm for real this time. I can't help it. I kind of want to be that bottle right now, gripped in that big hand and touching those full lips. I bet he tastes even better than he looks.

He notices my reaction, pinning me in a gaze that makes my heart thump hard against my ribcage. He's a wild animal scenting his prey. His nostrils flare, his steel blue eyes darkening. He leans toward me, bringing the rest of his face into focus.

Good gravy. He's Thor, without the giant hammer and cape. He's older than me, at least thirty-five or thirty-six.

"I haven't decided if I'm riding or not," I tell him, bringing my glass to my lips to take a greedy sip. It doesn't cool me down any.

"You afraid of a little challenge?"

"No."

"You sure about that, baby?"

Am I? I shrug, suddenly not so sure because I don't think he's talking about the bull. He's talking about me and him, I think. Because there is definitely something happening between us. I feel it like a gong striking in my soul. It's...terrifying. Getting stuck in your sports-bra after a shower when you're home alone terrifying.

I don't even know him, but I want to. He's different than anyone else I know, fascinating in ways my dad's friends will never be. They're all about their image and how they look. I don't think Jason Kirby gives a damn what anyone thinks about him.

"Why are you sitting all alone in the corner?" I ask when he gives me another of those half-smirks that do crazy things to my insides. My cheeks heat, but if he notices that I'm prying for intel, he doesn't call me out on it.

"Came alone," he says with a shrug, his eyes tracking back and forth across my face. "You?"

"Same."

He smirks at me. "You planning to leave alone, Miranda?"

"Maybe. You?" I take another sip of my water, trying to play it cool.

His smirk grows.

"What brings you here?" I ask. He stands out. Honestly, I think he'd stand out anywhere, but this doesn't look like his scene. He's too put together for a dive bar.

"Babysitting."

I wrinkle my nose. "Fun. Family?"

"Nah," he says, taking another pull from his bottle. "Some spoiled little rich girl and her friends. Guess my boss is trying to keep her safe and happy or some shit. I don't ask questions."

He shifts in the booth and then slides out, setting his beer on the table. Good lord, he is tall. I'm five six and he towers over me. He's also bigger than I thought. His broad shoulders block out the rest of the bar when he steps up in front of me. His thighs stretch the limits of his slacks.

He holds his hand out toward me. "Come on, Minnie."

"Where?" I ask...not that the answer seems to matter because I'm already slipping my hand into his and letting him pull me to my feet. My body grazes his and my nipples turn to hard little points. He smells like amber and wood smoke. The combination is decadent, delicious.

"Going to give you your first ride, baby."

Adore You is available now!

Nichole's Book Beauties

Want to connect with Nichole and other readers? We're building a girl gang! Join Nichole Rose's Book Beauties on Facebook for fun, games, and behind-the-scenes exclusives!

Instalove Book Club

The Instalove Book Club is now in session!

Get the inside scoop from your favorite instalove authors, meet new authors to love, and snag a free book and bonus content from featured authors every month. The Instalove Book Club newsletter goes out once per week!

Join the Club: http://instalovebookclub.com

Follow Nichole

Sign-up for Nichole's mailing list at http://authorni cholerose.com/newsletter to stay up to date on all new releases and for exclusive ARC giveaways from Nichole Rose.

Want to connect with Nichole and other readers? Join Nichole Rose's Book Beauties on Facebook!

facebook.com/AuthorNicholeRose/

instagram.com/AuthorNicholeRose

twitter.com/AuthNicholeRose

bookbub.com/authors/nichole-rose

tiktok.com/@authornicholerose

Also by Nichole Rose

<u>Her Alpha Series</u>
Her Alpha Daddy Next Door
Her Alpha Boss Undercover
Her Alpha's Secret Baby
Her Alpha Protector
Her Date with an Alpha
Her Alpha: The Complete Series

<u>Her Bride Series</u>
His Future Bride
His Stolen Bride
His Secret Bride
His Curvy Bride
His Captive Bride
His Blushing Bride
His Bride: The Complete Series

Claimed Series

Possessing Liberty

Teaching Rowan

Claiming Caroline

Kissing Kennedy

Claimed: The Complete Series

Love on the Clock Series

Adore You

Hold You

Keep You

Protect You

Love on the Clock: The Complete Series

The Billionaires' Club

The Billionaire's Big Bold Weakness

The Billionaire's Big Bold Wish

The Billionaire's Big Bold Woman

The Billionaire's Big Bold Wonder

The Billionaires' Club: The Complete Series

Playing for Keeps

Cutie Pie

Ice Breaker
Ice Prince
Ice Giant
Cold as Ice
Ice Storm (coming soon)

Full-Length Titles

Crash into You
Fight for You (coming soon)
Kill for You (coming soon)

The Second Generation

A Blushing Bride for Christmas

Love Bites

Come Undone
Dripping Pearls

Echoes of Forever

His Christmas Miracle
Taken by the Hitman
Wicked Saint

<u>The Ruined Trilogy</u>

Physical Science

Wrecked

Wanton

Wicked

<u>Destination Romance</u>

Romancing the Cowboy

Beach House Beauty

<u>Standalone Titles</u>

A Touch of Summer

Black Velvet

His Secret Obsession

Dirty Boy

Naughty Little Elf

Tempted by December

Devil's Deceit

A Bride for the Beast (writing with Fern Fraser)

A Hero for Her

Pretty Little Mess

Dear Mr. Dad Bod

Easy on Me
Easy Ride

Easy Surrender

One Night with You
Falling Hard

Model Behavior

Learning Curve

Angel Kisses

Silver Spoon MC
The Surgeon

The Heir

The Lawyer

The Prodigy

The Bodyguard

Silver Spoon MC Collection: Nichole's Crew

Silver Spoon Falls
Xavier's Kitten

Callum's Hope

Snow's Prince

Aurora's Knight

Silver Spoon Falcons
Leia's Playmaker
Aspen's Defense (coming soon)
Gabbi's Goalie (coming soon)

<u>**writing with Loni Ree as Loni Nichole**</u>
Dillon's Heart
Razor's Flame
Ryker's Reward
Zane's Rebel
Oral Arguments
Grizz's Passion
Garrett's Obsession

About Nichole Rose

Nichole Rose writes filthy, feel-good romance for curvy readers. Her books feature headstrong, sassy women and the alpha males who consume them. From grumpy detectives to country boys with attitude to instalove and over-the-top declarations, nothing is off-limits.

Nichole is sure to have a steamy, sweet story just right for everyone. She fully believes the world is ugly enough without trying to fit falling in love into a one-size-fits-all box.

When not writing, Nichole enjoys fine wine, cute shoes, and everything supernatural. She is happily married to the love of her life and is a proud mama to the world's most ridiculous fur-babies. She and her husband live in Arkansas.

You can learn more about Nichole and her books at authornicholerose.com.

facebook.com/AuthorNicholeRose/

instagram.com/AuthorNicholeRose

twitter.com/AuthNicholeRose

bookbub.com/authors/nichole-rose

tiktok.com/@authornicholerose

www.ingramcontent.com/pod-product-compliance
Lightning Source LLC
Chambersburg PA
CBHW052012150726

47999CB00004B/1626